"You're a Very Beautiful Woman, Megan . . .

More beautiful than I remembered," he whispered.

He was touching her, disturbing rational thought, and a small, but vital part of her exulted in the knowledge that he still wanted her. Her voice, a throaty whisper, was filled with the ache of raw emotions. "I don't think it would be wise to get involved again."

"Too late," he murmured, moving nearer to her. His breath whispered across her hair. "We're already involved. . . ."

Dear Reader:

Romance readers have been enthusiastic about Silhouette Special Editions for years. And that's not by accident: Special Editions were the first of their kind and continue to feature realistic stories with heightened romantic tension.

The longer stories, sophisticated style, greater sensual detail and variety that made Special Editions popular are the same elements that will make you want to read book after book.

We hope that you enjoy this Special Edition today, and will enjoy many more.

The Editors at Silhouette Books

LISA JACKSON
Innocent by Association

Silhouette Special Edition

Published by Silhouette Books New York

America's Publisher of Contemporary Romance

To Carol

Special thanks to Bruce Cramer

 SILHOUETTE BOOKS
300 E. 42nd. St., New York, N.Y. 10017

Copyright © 1985 by Susan Crose

Distributed by Pocket Books

ISBN: 0-373-09244-X

First Silhouette Books printing June 1985

10 9 8 7 6 5 4 3 2 1

America's Publisher of Contemporary Romance

Printed in the U.S.A.

BC91

LISA JACKSON

was raised in Molalla, Oregon, and now lives with her husband, Mark, and her two sons in a suburb of Portland, Oregon. Lisa and her sister, Natalie Bishop, who is also a Silhouette author, live within earshot of each other and do all their work in Natalie's basement. Lisa and Natalie are both represented in the Silhouette Special Edition list this month.

Books by Lisa Jackson

Silhouette Intimate Moments

Dark Side of the Moon #39
Gypsy Wind #79

Silhouette Special Editions

A Twist of Fate #118
The Shadow of Time #180
Tears of Pride #194
Pirate's Gold #215
A Dangerous Precedent #233
Innocent by Association #244

DENVER, COLORADO

1 17TH ST. FINANCIAL DISTRICT
"WALL STREET OF THE WEST"
2 LARIMER SQUARE

Chapter One

Another scandal would surely ruin her.

Megan shuddered, not from the cold, but from the sudden premonition of what was to come.

She could feel her teeth clenching together in determination, and her graceful jaw hardened almost imperceptibly as she realized that everything she had worked so painstakingly to accomplish was about to go down the drain.

The door opened. Megan managed a confident smile as she brushed a wayward wisp of copper-streaked hair out of her eyes and concentrated on the small, wiry man entering the prestigious office of the president of McKearn Investments.

She studied the intense expression on the face of Henry Silvas as the balding accountant rubbed his thin shock of white hair. From the deep furrow on Henry's forehead, Megan sensed trouble. More trouble than she had at first suspected. She had to fight to keep her shoulders from sagging as she met Henry's disturbed gaze.

"Evening," Henry muttered, removing his overcoat and taking a seat on the opposite side of the desk. He settled uncomfortably into the expensive wing chair and smiled tightly. "Where's the rest of the crew?"

"Everyone left at five tonight," Megan explained. "I thought it would be best if I saw you alone."

Silvas nodded and opened his briefcase. "Good idea."

A shiver of dread ran up Megan's spine. She frowned. "I assume that means that you have bad news."

Henry Silvas's small face puckered thoughtfully. "That remains to be seen." He shook his head as if he had encountered the first financial puzzle of his life that he hadn't been able to piece together.

"What do you mean?" Megan crossed her arms over her chest, leaned back in her chair and observed the small man with the reputation for being as sharp as the pencils he used. Henry Silvas was the best accountant Denver had to offer. His fee was stiff, but he was worth every cent. A no-nonsense individual known for his accuracy, Henry left no stone unturned in his audits of financial records. Megan's father had trusted Henry in the past, and Henry had proved himself to be worth his weight in gold.

"I mean that nothing in the internal workings of your office seems out of the ordinary . . . at least at first look."

"I know that much," Megan stated cautiously as she absently smoothed her sleek auburn hair away from her face. She could feel the hesitancy in the accountant's words.

Henry managed a thin smile and looked appreciatively into Megan's astute gaze. "And that's why you called me," he concluded with a shrewd smile.

Megan nodded, silently encouraging him to continue. Henry withdrew a cigar and rolled it between his thick fingers. "You don't miss much, do you, Meg?"

Her stern lips lifted a little at the corners. Henry Silvas wasn't one to hand out compliments casually. "I hope not," she admitted. "Now, tell me what you found." Before he could respond, she lifted her chin and cautioned him. "And don't pull any punches."

Henry's small dark eyes looked through thick glasses and studied the concern evidenced on Megan's face. Two points of color highlighted her cheekbones, and her smooth forehead was drawn into a concentrated frown. "Something bothers me," he admitted as he struck a match and held it to the end of the cigar.

"I knew it." Inclining her head, she met his worried gaze without any outward sign of the defeat she felt forming in the pit of her stomach. "What did you find?"

"Nothing I could put my finger on," Henry conceded with a shake of his balding head. "All of the books seem to be in perfect order . . . and the clients' accounts look good . . ."

"What then?" She had already guessed the answer but wanted his confirmation of the situation.

"It's some of the activity in the accounts," Henry replied with a frown. "It's good . . . maybe too good." His wise eyes narrowed into shrewd slits.

"I understand." Nervously, she ran her fingers along the gleaming oaken edge of her desk. "I trust you've got the proof to confirm your theory."

"Look at these." Henry extracted computer printouts from his briefcase. Megan recognized the names of the account holders on the September statements. A couple of the accounts were very large. Megan groaned inwardly, though she had expected the worst.

As Megan scanned the thick stack of statements, she noticed red marks with notations of dates on a few of the most lucrative trades. "What are these?" she asked solemnly while reaching for her glasses and studying Henry's notes. Her fingers skipped from one red mark on the paper to the next.

Henry retrieved an envelope of newspaper clippings from his briefcase and without comment handed the yellowed articles to the winsome president of McKearn Investments. Megan's clear gray eyes skimmed the clippings knowledgeably. Across each newspaper article, Henry had scrawled an angry red date. "Date of publication?" Megan asked without lifting her eyes from the incriminating scraps of paper.

"Um-hum."

Adjusting her reading glasses on her nose, Megan reread each of the clippings before comparing them to the statements of her clients. "All the articles are from the *Denver Financial Times*," she murmured to herself. Henry nodded thoughtfully and puffed on his cigar as the meaning of the evidence became clear to her. "These trades were made two days *before* the columns appeared in the paper." She took off her glasses, set them on the desk and pinched the bridge of her nose as she thought.

"You expected this, didn't you?"

"Yes," she whispered. "I just hoped that it wasn't true." A headache was beginning to throb at her temples. "Who was the broker?" she asked calmly, reopening her eyes. The look she gave Henry was coldly professional.

"George Samples," Henry supplied.

Megan nodded, having anticipated the accountant's response. "So he was in cahoots with someone at the *Times,* got the information before publication, made his trades and . . ."

". . . made a helluva lot of money for his clients."

"And himself as well, I'd venture to guess." Megan's eyes narrowed speculatively. "This is going to cause an incredible scandal," she predicted. "That's something I'd rather avoid."

"Because of your father's health?"

"That's one reason," Megan allowed. Her intelligent eyes searched the face of the small man sitting uncomfortably across from her. Henry lifted his eyebrows over the wire rims of his glasses.

"This is one helluva mess, Meg."

"You're telling me."

"It won't be long until the SEC gets wind of it."

Megan caught her lower lip between her teeth. Her thoughts were racing wildly through her mind.

"I know." She released a disgusted sigh and rose from her chair. "I just need a little time to break the news to Dad."

Henry frowned and shook his graying head. "Impossible. You'll have to take this to the SEC immediately. Your reputation, along with McKearn Investments', is at stake, you know." He considered the ash on the end of his cigar. "As for Samples, you've got no choice but to fire him."

"Gladly," Megan replied. George Samples had been a thorn in her side ever since her father's retirement.

"I'm sorry about all this, Meg."

"So am I."

Henry frowned at the printouts. "I did some checking," he said quietly.

"More?" Her black brows rose inquisitively.

"More than I had to . . . but I felt that I should because of everything your father did for me."

Megan nodded. The long-standing relationship between her father and Henry Silvas had spanned nearly twenty turbulent years.

"I took the liberty of checking out these accounts —the ones with the illegal trades."

"And what did you find?" For the first time since Henry had entered the room, Megan was uneasy. So far, she had suspected everything his audit confirmed. But the look in his myopic eyes gave her pause. There was more—something that didn't jibe with the rest.

"That's what bothers me," Henry confided. "There are only nine accounts involved, and from what I can gather, eight of the accounts are directly related to Samples—close friends, his fiancée, and even a dummy account that I suspect belongs to Samples himself."

"But . . . ?" Megan prodded, sifting through the papers scattered on the desk.

"The ninth one doesn't seem to fit." Henry stubbed out his cigar and retrieved the statement in question from his briefcase. He handed it to Megan.

Megan's breath caught in her throat and her heart seemed to drop to the floor. "Garrett Reaves," she murmured, reading from the front page of the statement. "You think he's involved?" Her gray eyes fastened on the worried face of the accountant, and somehow she managed to hide the fact that her poise was breaking into tiny fragments of the past.

Henry shrugged. "It looks that way."

"But why would Reaves be involved in anything like this? It doesn't make a lot of sense," she muttered, trying to consider the problem from a purely professional point of view and ignore the turbulent storm of emotions raging within her. Megan forced herself to appear indifferent despite the shadowed memories that threatened to distort her objectivity. She had to forget the solitary black weekend filled with raging storms of passion and pain . . .

"Why not?"

"Reaves Chemical is a very profitable organization," Megan pointed out, though her throat constricted at the memory of his betrayal three long years ago.

Henry seemed skeptical. He tented his fingers as he thought. "But Mr. Reaves doesn't own all of the stock."

"True, but—"

"And his divorce cost him a bundle."

Megan's dignity faltered for a heart-stopping instant. "That's only hearsay," she responded defensively.

Henry squinted and studied the condemning printout. "Maybe," he acknowledged.

"But you don't think so," she prodded, stifling the urge to shudder.

"Let's just say, I think it's highly coincidental." Henry heaved a worried sigh. "The thing of it is that one of the newspaper articles was on Reaves Chemical stock. Mr. Reaves made nearly a hundred thousand dollars on that trade alone."

"That's not unreasonable. He does control a large block of shares. He's a wealthy man." *Why was she protecting him? After all of the torture, why would she be so foolish as to try to defend him?*

"You think!"

"It's common knowledge," Megan replied, wondering at her uncharacteristic desire to protect his reputation. Garrett Reaves was a bastard, and by all reasonable accounts she should hate him.

In the few months since she had taken over as president of McKearn Investments, Garrett Reaves hadn't made an appearance at the small brokerage. But that was to be expected, considering the circumstances. Garrett didn't want to see her any more than she wanted to confront him. At Jed McKearn's request, when he had retired, George Samples had been given the lucrative Reaves account. And Megan had no reason to think that Garrett Reaves was unhappy with the situation.

Until now.

"Then why did he sell short on his own company's stock?" the feisty accountant demanded. "It just doesn't make much sense . . . unless maybe he was involved in this scam. It's not common practice for the majority stockholder to speculate on his own company's stock—and some of George's other 'special' accounts have made out on this same trade."

"I can't answer that one," Megan allowed reluctantly.

"And I'm willing to bet that our friend, Mr. Reaves, can't either."

"He's been out of the country for nearly a year. . . ."

Henry's bushy gray brows quirked. "Not all of the time. From what I understand, the chemical plant in Japan is just about operational." He paused thoughtfully, for dramatic effect. "And it wouldn't be the first time that an executive issued orders for something illegal from foreign soil."

"I suppose you're right," she conceded with a reluctant shrug of her shoulders. Henry's logic was impossible to refute. "But it's hard for me to think of him as a crook."

"I know." Henry's small eyes softened. "Reaves was close to Patrick." At the mention of her brother's name, Megan stiffened and her face paled. The sudden change in her bearing wasn't lost on the accountant. Henry's soft palms turned upward. "Look, Meg, there's a chance that Reaves isn't involved in this mess . . . but it's a slim one. And you can't afford to wait to find out. Leave that up to the SEC and save your neck, for Pete's sake. If Reaves is innocent, he'll be able to prove it. Right now you have a duty and an obligation to the rest of your clients . . . as well as to your father."

"Then you think I should call Ted Benson."

Henry nodded at the mention of the attorney's name. "If you can't get through to Benson, talk to one of his partners, but you'd better do it before the SEC comes breathing down your neck. Let the lawyers battle it out."

As Megan saw the situation, she had no choice. *If only Garrett weren't involved.* From her standing position, she reached for the phone, just barely managing to hide the fact that her hands were beginning to shake. "Thanks, Henry," she said with a tight smile.

"Don't thank me," he replied. "You're in for the fight of your life." Henry noticed the flicker of sadness in her large gray eyes, and he hated himself for being the one who'd had to confirm her suspicions.

"Don't I know it," she whispered as she removed her earring and balanced the phone on her shoulder before dialing the law offices of Benson and Tate. "God, I hate to do this," she murmured, thinking of a thousand reasons, mostly concerning Garrett Reaves, to put off the call.

Henry left the reports on the desk and snapped his briefcase closed. "I'll talk to you later in the week," he said as he rose from the chair and walked out of the room. Megan watched as the heavy wooden door closed silently behind his wiry form.

No one answered at the law firm. Megan replaced the receiver and removed her reading glasses. She shivered as if from a sudden blast of cold air. "Why, Garrett?" she wondered aloud as she stood away from the desk and placed her arms protectively across her breasts.

Darkness had begun to shadow the city as the vivid image of the one man she had vowed to hate raced wantonly through her mind. How long had it been since she'd last seen him—a year?

As the painful memories resurfaced, she pressed her lips together in determination and reached for the phone. Forcing her thoughts away from Garrett, she dialed the offices of Benson and Tate again. After nine rings, a gruff-sounding legal assistant answered the phone and promised to have Ted Benson return Megan's call.

"That's that," Megan whispered to herself as she hung up and stared sightlessly out of the window. Dusk had begun to settle over Denver, and the brilliant lights of the Sixteenth Street Mall began to illuminate that section of the mile-high city. From her position on the eighth floor of the Jefferson Tower, Megan had a panoramic view of the business district. But neither the city nor the shadowy Rocky

Mountains in the distance held any interest for her tonight.

With a weary sigh, she tapped her fingers restlessly on the cool windowpane. "Dear Lord, Garrett, I hope you're not involved in this mess," Megan whispered before turning out the lights and locking the doors of the office.

Chapter Two

The board of directors of McKearn Investments had begrudgingly appointed Megan to fill the vacant position of president of the small brokerage house. At the time, no one had suspected that Jed McKearn's condition would deteriorate, and the stodgy members of the board, along with Megan herself, had believed that Jed would soon return to oversee the operation.

With only a few grumblings and undisguised looks of disapproval, the board members had unanimously accepted Jed's proposal to let Megan sit in her father's prestigious office and helm the course of McKearn Investments. After all, it was only temporary, and Megan had paid her dues. An M.B.A. from Stanford and three years as Jed's assistant gave her all the credibility she needed, and it didn't hurt that her last name happened to be McKearn.

If she had followed her own instincts and let George Samples go six months ago, she possibly could have avoided the scandal that Henry Silvas had uncovered. She called herself every kind of fool for not striding out of that initial board meeting and resigning on the spot. The presidency had been granted her with a burdensome restriction: Every major decision within the company had to be approved by her father. And now she was paying for it.

As Megan leaned against the cool panes of the office window the morning after her meeting with Henry Silvas, her small hands curled into fists of frustration and she rapped one soundly on the frosted glass. How could she have let this happen? She closed her eyes in disgust. And to think that Garrett Reaves might be involved. Her stomach knotted painfully when she considered the fact that Garrett's name was tied into the scam. Was he part of the swindle—or an innocent victim? Henry's evidence strongly suggested that Garrett had taken a chance—and gotten caught. It wouldn't be the first time.

The news would kill her father.

Last night, after hearing Henry's report, Megan had visited her parents. However, she had been unable to broach the subject of the scam with her father; Jed had suffered a tiring day at the clinic. Megan's mother, after tearfully confiding to her daughter that Jed's condition seemed to worsen with each passing day, had asked Megan not to disturb him. Megan had respected her mother's wishes and had postponed telling Jed about Henry Silvas's audit. All in all, it had been a lousy day that had darkened into a long, sleepless night.

Megan didn't expect this morning to be much of an improvement.

George Samples breezed into the room with his usual swagger, and somehow Megan managed a tight smile for his benefit.

"You wanted to see me?" he asked, nervously rubbing his fingers along his jaw and touching the corners of his thin, clipped moustache as he dropped into one of the side chairs near the window.

Megan took her chair on the opposite side of the desk. She didn't mince words. "Henry Silvas came to see me last evening."

George looked expectant. Megan could almost hear the *so what?* forming in the young broker's cagey mind.

"He brought these with him." Megan slid the marked copies of the September statements and the faded clippings from the *Denver Financial Times* across the oak surface of the desk.

George retrieved the evidence indifferently before shrugging his shoulders and adjusting the crease in one of the legs of his tailored wool slacks. "What's all this?" His gold eyes slid down the clippings without interest.

"It's proof of a scam, George," Megan began, and then, very patiently, never allowing her white-hot temper to surface, she told him about her meeting with Henry Silvas.

She attempted to give George the benefit of the doubt and allow him to present his side of the story, but George refused to answer her questions rationally. As she spoke, she noticed the flush of anger rise on George's face.

When Megan painstakingly explained the evidence mounting against him, the brash young broker lost the thin thread of control he had over his volatile temper.

"You've been planning this from the first day you took over your old man's job," George accused, his thin lips drawing into an insolent line. His legs were crossed and his right foot was bouncing erratically while his surging rage got the better of him. "This story about a scam is just an excuse to get rid of me!"

Megan's steadfast gray eyes never wavered, not for an instant. What George was suggesting was ridiculous. They both knew it. "You know me better than that, George," she insisted quietly.

"Henry Silvas has a reputation for destroying people," George returned with a narrowing gaze. "Boy, have you been conned. I wonder who Silvas is covering up for?"

Megan shook her head slowly, and her round, gray eyes remained clear. "I studied the audit—"

"Sure you did," George scoffed.

A light rap on the door interrupted Megan's response as Jenny, the receptionist, poked her head into the room. "I'm sorry to bother you," the young girl apologized, "but Ted Benson is on line one."

At the mention of the attorney's name, George visibly paled. Until then, he had thought that Megan was bluffing.

Megan noticed George's discomfort. "That's all

right, Jenny. I'll take the call," Megan said to the girl, signaling an end to her meeting with George.

Jenny escaped from the strained room, and Megan's hand paused expectantly over the telephone receiver. Her intense gray eyes looked into the wrathful expression of George Samples. The young man's brow was creased with anger and worry. Small beads of perspiration had collected in the thin strands of his reddish moustache. His small gold eyes were shadowed in dark circles and they darted frantically from Megan to the telephone and back again.

"So this is it?" he demanded, using a new tack, hoping to appeal to the kinder side of her nature. "You're really going to fire me? I can't believe it."

"Believe it," Megan replied, and then softened her position slightly. "I'd prefer to think of your departure as a leave of absence until everything is cleared up. And, if I'm wrong about this, you'll have your job back with a sincere apology."

George laughed without any trace of humor. "Wonderful," he muttered sarcastically. "And what will I do in the meantime? God Almighty, I should have known you would fall for a story like this. Well, I just want to be the first to tell you that someone else is behind this scam! Not me! I've worked too many years for this company to throw them away on a lousy swindle the likes of this." His feet dropped noisily to the floor. "You can call it anything you like, but I've been framed!" His eyes narrowed spitefully as he cast Megan one final, vindictive glance before marching out of her office.

Megan waited until George had left the room and then removed her earring before cradling the phone between her shoulder and ear. As she had expected, Ted Benson had grown tired of waiting and had hung up. Megan quickly dialed the number for the legal offices of Benson and Tate.

The rest of the day passed quickly. Megan was caught in the middle of a whirlwind of meetings, telephone conversations and paperwork. The only blessing in an otherwise distressing day was that, as yet, the press hadn't found out about the scam. Unfortunately, it was only a matter of time before the hungry reporters would be collecting within the building. Once the story got out, all hell would break loose. And, no doubt, for the first time in three years, she would come face-to-face with the one man who could cruelly twist her heart until she bled.

The hours flew by. Ted Benson had convinced her that he had the situation well in control. Megan managed to call an emergency board meeting, which was scheduled for the next day. And throughout all of the activity, her thoughts lingered on Garrett. It was as if that single, darkly passionate weekend still bound her mercilessly to him. Patrick's accident might have severed the tangible ties between Megan and Garrett, but it couldn't destroy the intangible emotions that still surrounded her heart. "You're a fool," she chastised herself angrily, and tried to force her concentration back to her notes for tomorrow's board meeting.

George Samples had left her office right after his

morning confrontation with Megan, and she was surprised to see him back at his desk later in the day. Megan had assumed that her discussion with George was finished. But she was wrong.

It was nearly closing time when Megan passed by George's desk. Only he and a few other workers were still in the office. A dark frown creased George's face as he slid insolent eyes up Megan's body.

"You've been against me since day one," the brash young broker charged unexpectedly. Megan was forced to pause at his desk and respond to the accusation.

"You know that's not true," Megan replied, keeping her voice down and her composure intact. "I've given you every possible break." Her steely gray eyes withstood his furious attack, and she managed a sincere smile. "If you'd like to discuss this further, let's go into my office—"

"You'd like that, wouldn't you?" George cut in. "We wouldn't want to let the rest of the staff get wind of all of this . . . would we?"

"George, I think we should talk this over."

"You don't want to discuss anything. You're just looking for an excuse to shut me up." The pompous Yale graduate smiled condescendingly.

"I'm trying to reason with you."

"Ha! You don't know the meaning of the word, Ms. McKearn. Reasoning with you is impossible. It always has been. And I'm tired of taking all of your crap."

Megan realized the situation was irreconcilable. "I'll have the accounting department give you a check for a month's severance pay." She attempted to keep her anger under control. Hoping to prevent speculation by the other employees, who couldn't help but overhear the heated conversation, Megan stepped away from George's desk.

"Just like that, huh?"

"George, I can't keep you on, you know that. I can't even give you a letter of recommendation until this whole business is straightened out."

His sharp eyes accused her of a lie. "Well, what happens when the SEC proves me innocent? What then?"

"I'll be the first person to admit that I was wrong."

"But until then, you're satisfied to kick me out."

"I don't have any other choice."

George placed his fists on his hips. "Isn't that just like a woman!"

Megan's temper flared. "Being a woman has nothing to do with my decision."

"Sure it doesn't," he sneered, while opening his briefcase and stuffing the contents of his desk into it.

"I'm sure my father would do the same thing—"

"Oh, give me a break, will you? You've never been able to hold a candle to the old man! Even that louse of a brother of yours could have run this firm better than you have. Damn, but this company took a nosedive when you took over."

The crack about Patrick hit a sensitive raw nerve. "That's enough," Megan warned, her eyes wide with indignation and authority.

"You're right on that count, Ms. McKearn. *It is enough!* I've had it with this two-bit operation!" With his final, vindictive comment, George snapped his briefcase closed, jerked it off his desk and marched angrily past the desks of his co-workers. When he pushed open the glass door separating the brokerage firm from the rest of the building, the panes rattled in their frames.

Some of the other brokers who had witnessed the argument turned their confused gazes back to the work on their desks. Though she could feel the muscles in her back stiffen, Megan forced a confident but tight smile to those employees who caught her eye before she picked up the reports for which she had been searching and carried them back to her office.

"What a day," she murmured to herself as she sat down at her desk. "And it's only going to get worse." Firing George hadn't been easy, but the other tasks she had to face were just as ominous.

She still had to confront her father with Henry's audit and the possible SEC investigation. Despite his illness, Jed McKearn wouldn't want to hear excuses from his daughter, and he would expect Megan to take the proper action to squelch the scandal before it started. The worst part of it was that he wouldn't enjoy hearing what she intended to tell the board members in the meeting tomorrow.

There was also the problem of the clients whose accounts were involved in George's scheme. Pending the legal confrontation between the attorneys and the SEC, the accounts had to be carefully watched. Ted Benson, as attorney for McKearn Investments, had promised to contact each of the account holders. Once again, Megan's wayward thoughts turned to Garrett. Had Ted been able to reach him by phone, or would Garrett receive a crisp letter from the offices of Benson and Tate? Megan knew as well as anyone that Garrett could be merciless in pursuing that which he desired; and yet, she doubted Reaves's participation in the swindle. If he had a reputation for being ruthless in the chemical industry, Megan attributed it to the fact that he had been a poor kid from Seattle who had made his fortune by combining luck with intelligence and pushing his way to the top. Megan had always felt respect whenever she heard the name Garrett Reaves.

Until that one black weekend, nearly three years ago, when her life had been shattered as easily as a crystal goblet.

Megan sighed wearily as she gazed at her cluttered desk. She picked up the scattered pages of Henry Silvas's audit and tapped them lightly on the polished wood before placing the neatly typed documents into her briefcase. She couldn't put it off any longer. She had to tell her father what was happening.

She felt the intrusion a second before it occurred. The door to her office was thrust open so violently that it thudded against the polished cherry wood paneling and the noise caught Megan off guard. She raised her head questioningly to face the cause of the disruption and found herself staring into the furious hazel eyes of Garrett Reaves.

Megan's throat constricted. Only once before had she seen such indignant wrath storming in a man's glare. The undisguised fury contorted his features and pierced through her composure just as it had in the past.

Reaves stopped in the doorway; he had hoped that there would be someone of authority in Jed McKearn's office, and he was sadly disappointed. The one person he hadn't expected to face was Jed's daughter, Megan, and the sight of her sitting defiantly behind Jed's oak desk made him hesitate—if only for a second.

Though Garrett knew that Megan was running the investment firm, he had understood that her position of president was temporary. George Samples had hinted that Megan was leaving the brokerage house because of some as yet undisclosed scandal, and that Jed was replacing his daughter. Obviously George's information was wrong, or Jed hadn't yet cleaned house.

Whatever the reason, Megan was here, staring accusingly at him with the same wide, dove gray eyes that had touched a dangerous part of him in the past. Her face was still as elegantly sculpted as he remembered, and her flawless skin remained unlined.

Megan slowly rose from the desk and swallowed against the lump of wounded pride rising in her throat. The moment she had been anticipating and dreading had come.

Garrett's thick black hair was disheveled, as if it had been carelessly blown by the wind. He didn't seem to notice. His angular face and craggy, masculine features were drawn into a frown of angry resentment. Heavy black brows, pulled into an uncompromising scowl, guarded glinting eyes that were more green than brown. Those eyes watched every movement on Megan's even features, accusing her of conspiring against him.

Megan felt the involuntary stiffening of her spine as she straightened to face him, and she noted that his considerable frame in the doorway left little space for Jenny, the petite receptionist, to squeeze through.

"I'm sorry, Ms. McKearn—I couldn't stop him," Jenny announced as she cast Garrett Reaves a perturbed look.

"It's all right, Jenny," Megan replied, not lifting her cool gaze from the famous face of the man standing angrily in the doorway. Three years of her life seemed to melt into the shadowed corners of the room.

Megan had to remind herself that Reaves Chemical was one of Denver's largest industries. Garrett Reaves's face was often photographed to complement stories about the chemical company in the business section of the *Denver Financial Times*.

"Come in, Mr. Reaves, please," Megan said stiffly, and noted that his dark brows quirked at her formality. She motioned toward one of the chairs near her desk. "Take a seat. Can I have Jenny bring you a cup of coffee?" Surprisingly, though her heart was pounding furiously, a modicum of her professional aplomb remained with her.

Garrett eyed Megan suspiciously. His stormy hazel eyes narrowed in thought. "I just want to know what the hell's going on here," he replied, ignoring her polite offer. His voice was low and calm, despite the intensity of his words or his insinuation that something of outlandish proportions was wrong.

Every muscle in his body tensed as he stood in the

doorway, and it was evident to Megan that his anger was about to explode.

Meeting his furious glare without giving evidence of any of her own storming emotions, Megan placed her glasses on the bridge of her nose and nodded thoughtfully. The last thing she wanted was a confrontation with the one man who could cut her to the bone. With one malicious word to the press, he could start the first whispers of a scandal that would certainly ruin her professionally. And that didn't begin to touch what he could do to her personally. Once before he had left her life in a shambles. No doubt he could do it again.

"I'm sure you do," she agreed softly. "We have a lot to discuss. . . ." Her cool gray eyes left him to rest on the small receptionist. "I can handle this, Jenny. See that Mr. Reaves and I aren't disturbed."

"It's about time to lock up," the pert redhead nervously reminded Megan.

Glancing at the antique clock mounted on the bookcase, Megan confirmed Jenny's remark. The long day was about over. Thank God. "You're right," she murmured. "Would you please lock the doors behind you when you leave? I'll show Mr. Reaves out."

The young girl nodded, and after sliding another ungrateful look in Garrett's direction, Jenny walked out of the room. When the door closed behind the receptionist, Garrett crossed the plush carpet of Megan's office in three swift strides. His condemning gaze swept over the interior of the room before coming to rest on Megan's wary face. The desk was the battle line. It seemed little barrier against Garrett's raging anger.

"I'm waiting," he announced, pulling at his tie before pressing his palms onto the wood, curling his fingers over the edge of the desk and leaning toward Megan. His square jaw was thrust defiantly close to her face.

"For?"

"An explanation," he replied, his eyes blazing with fury. "What's going on, Megan?" he demanded. "Why the hell are you trying to frame me?"

"I'm not," she stated without hesitation. "It seems as if you're doing a good enough job of that on your own."

Withholding the urge to pound his fist on the desk, Garrett pushed his rugged face nearer to hers. She could feel the heat of his breath on her cheeks. His dark eyes scrutinized her with such intensity that she had to force herself to hold her ground and return his unyielding stare.

"If you'll just take a seat—"

"I want answers, lady," he cut in, ignoring her request, "and I want them *now!*"

"I'll answer anything I can. However, I think it would behoove you to talk to Ted Benson."

"I already have."

"Then you understand my position—"

"Cut the crap, Megan. What're you trying to do? George Samples told me my account's being audited."

"It's only temporary," Megan replied. "Until the SEC—"

"The SEC! What the devil are you talking about?" His anger was replaced by incredulity. Shaking his head as if he didn't understand a word she was saying, he raked his fingers through his ebony hair and let out a disgusted breath of air.

"If you'll just give me a chance to explain, I'll be glad to tell you," she retorted, hiding the pain in her heart at being so near him again.

He looked suddenly weary, as if he hadn't slept in days. Megan sensed that what little patience he held on to was wearing precariously thin. In three years, Garrett had aged. Small lines webbed attractively near the corners of his eyes, softening the hard, angular planes of his face. A few strands of gray stood out against his otherwise dark hair, lending a quiet dignity to his rough features.

"I'm sorry," he said without meaning. "By all means, explain this fiasco to me."

Garrett studied the power and confidence in Megan's eyes. He noticed the regal tilt of defiance in her elegant chin and the refined manner in which her flawless skin stretched softly over her lofty cheekbones. Her inquisitive black brows were arched at him in sophisticated challenge. If she still had any feelings for him whatsoever, she hid them well.

"For starters, let me assure you that there is no fiasco—not so far as McKearn Investments is involved."

He didn't bother to hide his disbelief. "No? Then would you mind telling me exactly why the funds in my account are a part of this mess, whatever the hell it is?"

"I'm attempting to."

"Then let's get on with it." He couldn't conceal the impatience in his voice or the fatigued slump of his shoulders as he settled into one of the chairs near her desk. He leaned his head against the stiff back of the chair, and his eyes roved restlessly around the interior of the room.

The entire office was decorated in deference to her femininity. Though the room still had the air of a business office, the masculine trappings of Jed Mc-Kearn had been replaced with Tiffany lamps, royal blue wing chairs and leather-bound editions of classical literature. Gone were the scent of stale cigar smoke and the unspoken invitation of a drink before business was discussed. Now the room held the faint fragrance of freshly cut flowers and a provocative hint of perfume. The same fragrance that had haunted his nights for the last three years. . . .

Garrett pulled his wandering thoughts back into perspective. He was positive that the changes made at McKearn Investments in the last year and a half were not to his advantage. And he didn't like the new atmosphere in this office. It disturbed him and reminded him of a time he would rather forget. He was usually a strong man who made decisions easily, but there was something about Megan McKearn that got to him. There always had been.

It was more than her beauty. It was the fire in her gray eyes and the air of feminine mystique that attracted him and made him cautious. When Garrett first met Megan, he had noticed the regal tilt of her head, the pride in her rigid back and the mystery in her wide gray eyes. Her allure had nearly been his undoing.

Carefully veiled now behind thick glasses and a severe hairstyle, Megan's intriguing femininity was still present. It had beckoned him in the past and still touched him. It was a temptation he had persistently avoided and would continue to avoid. Several years ago he had vowed to stay away from beautiful women. Until this moment, staring face-to-face with Megan, he had never been tempted to break that fateful promise to himself.

He smiled as if at a private irony. "Look, Megan, I've just spent two weeks out of the country. The last twelve hours have been divided between airports and airplanes. I'd like to get this over with so I can go home."

"Then I'll explain it to you as best I can." Peeking over the rims of her glasses, Megan managed what she hoped was a patient smile. She was convinced that the other account holders who had gained from George Samples's scheme had known about the scam from the beginning. Garrett Reaves was another case altogether.

His green-gold eyes clashed with hers, and Megan found it difficult to believe that he was involved in something as unscrupulous as fraud. He was a sensual man, and part of that sensuality came from the honesty in his stare. If she didn't remember her past so vividly, she would be tempted to believe that Garrett was innocent.

"McKearn Investments is currently involved in an investigation by the SEC." Before he might get the wrong idea, she continued, "This is no reflection on the brokerage house itself, you understand, but rather on the actions of one broker, his clients and a financial journal."

"Let me guess," Garrett interjected grimly. "The broker must be George Samples."

"Right—"

"And, therefore, my account is just naturally a part of the investigation." He tented his hands under his chin; his knowing eyes never left her face.

"This isn't just idle conjecture," she insisted.

"Of course not. It's guilt by association. Just because my broker of record is George Samples, you assume that I'm involved." His lips thinned menacingly as if he were appalled at the injustice of the situation.

"Not all of George's accounts were involved—"

"Just mine?" he accused, his voice rising. A small muscle in the corner of his jaw began to work, and his fingertips whitened with the increased pressure as he pushed his hands together.

"There were several," Megan said. "One of them was yours."

"Great!" Disgust was evident in his voice. He shook his dark head as if he couldn't believe what he was hearing. "Just what I need!" He dragged his suspicious eyes away from her face for a moment and sighed, as if to regain some of his diminishing restraint.

"The attorney promised that the SEC will complete the investigation as quickly as possible—"

"How the hell can he speak for the SEC? I don't have time to waste while I wait for a government agency to plow through your records and figure out that I'm not a part of this thing, whatever the hell it is." Once again his dark, knowing eyes assailed her. "I'm going to need most of the funds in my account by late December, and I'm not about to sit idle while McKearn Investments and the Securities and Exchange Commission try to blame me for something I didn't even know about."

"That's your prerogative," Megan stated, sensing that the tight rein on his anger was slipping and knowing intuitively that the full force of his wrath was something she had to avoid at all costs. She had witnessed his rage in the past, and his reputation for being unmerciful in business preceded him. McKearn Investments couldn't afford to have Garrett Reaves as an enemy. Nor could she. The scandal would be vicious enough without the added weight of Garrett's animosity.

"I think that the best way for us to handle this . . . problem is for you to release the funds in my account," he suggested.

"Certainly. In the morning—"

"Now!" Emphasis was added to his words by the dark shadows of mistrust in his eyes.

"Impossible."

His smile was without humor. "Certainly you've been in business long enough to realize that nothing's impossible." Savage eyes cut into her. He put his hands on the arms of his chair and pushed himself to his full height. "Maybe you don't understand me, Ms. McKearn: I'm closing my account."

"In the morning. *After* I've talked to Ted Benson."

His fists clenched and relaxed. "It's *my* money!"

"And right now it could well be under investiga-

tion by the SEC!" Megan stood, her face held high
to meet the challenge in his intense hazel eyes. "You
can't expect me to go against the advice of my
attorney." Her hands clenched in frustration.
"Look, my hands are tied." Her gray eyes darkened
ominously. "Perhaps you should take my suggestion
and call Ted Benson." She gestured with her palm
toward the phone.

"I'm talking to you, Megan." His palm slapped
the desk. "You're the president of this brokerage.
It's your responsibility to see that my interests are
protected. If an employee of McKearn Investments
is involved in anything shady, then your reputation is
on the line, not mine! Your father recommended
George Samples to me in the first place. Because of
Jed's recommendation, I assumed that Samples was
a man of integrity."

"We all did," Megan admitted.

"And apparently you were wrong." The hard line
of his mouth remained rigid.

Megan was noncommittal. Instinctively she sensed
that if she were to be drawn any further into the
argument, Garrett might use it against her later.
Though he hadn't mentioned the possibility of a
lawsuit, she could read the insinuations and warnings in the shadows of his gaze. "We'll see."

Garrett's eyes sparked with fury. "That we will,
Ms. McKearn," he threatened dangerously. "That
we will."

He strode out of the small office without so much
as a glance over his shoulder. Megan waited until the
office door swung shut behind him before she lowered herself into her chair.

The poise to which she had been desperately clinging escaped her and she let out a tired sigh. *Dear God, how had everything gotten so out of control? And why did Garrett have to be involved?* Involuntarily, she shuddered. Closing her eyes, she refused to release the tears of anger burning against her eyelids. Instead, she reached up and removed the pins holding the tight coil of auburn hair tightly in place. The long copper-colored waves tumbled free of their bond to rest in tangled disarray on her slim shoulders. Hoping to relieve some of the tension from the long afternoon, she set her glasses on the desk and ran her fingers through the thick strands surrounding her small, proud face.

Megan knew that she shouldn't let the threat of another scandal unnerve her. And she couldn't afford to let Garrett's presence as a man get to her. She realized that the knots twisting in her stomach weren't so much because of what she was about to face, but because of the past. Memories, fresh with senseless pain, surfaced in her weary mind.

To fight the tears of anguish forming in her eyes, Megan pressed her eyelids shut and swallowed. "I can't think about it . . . not now," she whispered to herself as she wiped away the tears.

The sound of the door opening once again caught her attention, and she looked up to find Garrett staring at her. For an embarrassing moment, Megan lost control of herself and her battered pride faltered.

The anger on his hard features faded as he witnessed the quiet pain in her large gray eyes. She cleared her throat, and when she spoke her voice was only a whisper. "Is there something I can do for you?" she asked as she recaptured a portion of her fleeing composure.

"Megan . . . I didn't mean . . ."

She forced determination into the proud tilt of her chin. The softness in her eyes disappeared. "There's no need to apologize," she assured him, although the sound of her name as he had spoken it caused her elegant brows to lift and her heart to miss a beat.

He took a step toward her, then halted. "Then I'd appreciate it if you would unlock the door."

"The door?" she repeated before realizing what he was talking about. "Oh . . . of course," she replied, hastily reaching into her purse for her key ring. She chided herself for forgetting that she had asked the receptionist to lock the front door of the office.

As she stood, she picked up her briefcase and tossed her raincoat over her arm. Garrett followed her into the reception area, and though she didn't look in his direction when she unlocked the door, she could feel him standing disturbingly close to her.

"We don't have to be on opposite sides of the issue, you know," he suggested, pondering the curve of her neck and leaning against the tempered glass separating the office from the corridor.

"I don't think we are," she replied. His thick brows cocked dubiously. "As far as I'm concerned, you're still a client of McKearn Investments."

"That's all?"

"That's all," she lied.

"Except that I have no control over the privacy of my account," he pointed out.

"For the time being."

He touched her arm just as she pushed the plate-glass door open. At the intimacy of the gesture, she lifted her eyes and stepped backward. There was something boldly masculine about him that she couldn't define, something powerfully male and overwhelming.

"I don't like the feeling that I'm not in control of what is mine," he said.

"I understand." She had only to remember the past.

"And I won't let it rest," he warned, stepping into the hallway of the building. "Not until everything's settled. Whatever this crime is that you think I committed, you're wrong, Megan, and I intend to do everything in my power to prove it!"

"That's your right," Megan said evenly, wondering just how far he would go with his threats.

"And if I have to, I'll sue McKearn Investments."

"I hope we can avoid a legal dispute." Her voice remained calm, and she managed to hide the desperation beginning to inch up her spine. *A lawsuit!* The publicity and scandal would destroy everything she had worked for.

"It's all up to you, Megan."

"Then perhaps we can talk it out."

"I tried that already," he stated, his eyes narrowing. "In your office. It didn't work."

"There's nothing I can do . . ."

Garrett noticed the trace of hopelessness in her voice. When he had walked back into her office he had been stunned at the sight of her, intrigued by the raw vulnerability in the beautiful oval of her face.

Three years of his life seemed to have disappeared into the night.

In an instant she had regained her composure, but just for a fleeting moment he had captured a glimpse of the woman he remembered. Quickly she had disguised her feelings. It occurred to him that she might be hiding something else as well. He decided to gamble.

His face hardened with ruthless determination. "Then I'll call my attorney tonight. No doubt you'll hear from him in the morning."

Megan's throat became tight with dread. "If you think you must—"

"Damn it, lady, you don't give me much of a choice, do you?" he said, looking toward the ceiling as if hoping for divine intervention. "You won't bother to talk this out logically, and then you back me up against the wall. What the hell do you expect from me?"

"Just a little time and patience," she replied, hoping her smile looked more convincing than it felt.

"A little time and patience?" he repeated, the corners of his mouth quirking as if he couldn't believe what he was hearing. "You've got my money, the S.E.C. is probably digging through the records of my account and God only knows what else . . . in fact, you're acting like I'm some kind of criminal or something, and you expect me to be patient?"

"I guess I forgot that patience isn't exactly your long suit."

Garrett's jaw tightened and he looked pointedly at his watch. "Something tells me that I'm not going to get hold of Ron Thurston now." His dark eyes rose to bore into hers.

"Probably not," Megan agreed. She checked the urge to wince at the prominent attorney's name. "Unless I bother him at home, I doubt if I can get in touch with him until tomorrow morning."

Megan inclined her head in mute agreement.

"So what are you going to do about it?"

"There's nothing—"

This time his hand reached out and gripped her shoulder. "Look, Megan, I don't want to hear any more canned speeches about the fact that your hands are tied because of the SEC. The reason I'm in this mess in the first place is because of your boy, George Samples." The fingers tightened over the soft muscles of her shoulder, and she could feel the warmth of his insistent touch through her jacket. "Now, as I see it, your firm *owes* me the benefit of the doubt."

Only a small space separated her upturned face from his. Demanding hazel eyes drilled into hers. "That's probably true," she conceded reluctantly.

"Then give it to me, damn it!"

"What do you suggest I do?"

He released his grip on her shoulder, and he clenched his fists in frustration. "I wish I knew." He raked impatient fingers through his hair as he thought. "Why don't you try telling me exactly what it is I'm up against," he suggested. "I haven't the slightest idea what all of this is about."

Megan calculated the risks and decided that it would be in the best interests of McKearn Investments to help Garrett Reaves. Despite her personal feelings for the man, he was an account holder, and there was the slight chance that he was, as he so vehemently claimed, innocent. If, however, he gave her any indication that he was involved with the scam, she would have no further obligation to him. She couldn't jeopardize the reputation of McKearn Investments. Her tight smile relaxed.

"I'll be glad to go over everything with you," she stated.

"Now?"

"I'd rather have Ted Benson with me."

His dark eyes sparked. "Out of the question. I want answers tonight."

Megan didn't hesitate. "I'll try to get hold of Ted. Perhaps we can meet you later. There are a few things I have to take care of first."

Garrett eyed her suspiciously, as if he thought she might run out on him. But something in her cool gaze convinced him that she would be true to her word. And why not? He held the trump card. He knew how desperate she was to avoid any bad publicity.

"Good." Once again his eyes darted to the watch on his cocked wrist before returning to her face. "Then I'll see you . . . when? About eight?"

"I'll be here," she assured him, relieved that the confrontation with the president of Reaves Chemical was drawing to a close, if only temporarily. She needed time and distance away from the disturbing man with the piercing hazel eyes.

"Not here," he stated, pushing on the door.

"Pardon me?"

"I'll expect you at my house. You remember the address?"

Megan's heart missed a beat. "I doubt that Mr. Benson will be inclined to drive to Boulder tonight."

Dark eyes sparked with green fire. "Convince him. Or come alone. I really don't give a damn how you arrange it."

"I'd feel more comfortable here, where I have access to all of the records."

"Bring them with you. Believe it or not, I have other things that I'd rather do than run back and forth to this office. I've been out of town for two weeks. Before coming here, I checked in at the office after landing at Stapleton. That's when I found out that all hell had broken lose. Now, I know it might not be convenient for you, but I really don't care. I want to go home, shower, change and answer some rather extensive correspondence that's been stacking up while I was gone. I think, in view of what's happening around here, that's not too much to ask."

She silently weighed the alternatives. There were none. Garrett had control and they both knew it. "I'll see you around eight."

There was a satisfied gleam in his dark eyes, as if he had just won a small victory and was savoring the sweetness of the conquest. Megan had the uneasy feeling that she had fallen very neatly into a well-executed seduction.

As she watched him stride to the elevators, Megan realized that he would stop at nothing to prove himself right—whether he was innocent or not.

Chapter Three

*M*egan's father was a man of conflicting impulses: strong-willed to the point of ruthlessness in business, but also a man of tender emotions for his family. Megan knew that she had never lived up to his expectations for her. Jed McKearn was from the old school of thought, and he considered Megan's independent streak a character flaw. He had made no bones about the fact that all he wanted from his hot-tempered daughter was a successful son-in-law and several grandchildren he could pamper.

As for the business, Jed had considered his son, Patrick, as the only rightful heir to McKearn Investments. All of his life Jed had worked to see that his son was well groomed for his intended position as president of the investment firm.

In both cases, Jed's ambitions for his children had been thwarted by fate. And now it was Megan's cursed independent streak that had allowed her to run the company.

Megan was sure the irony of the situation escaped her father. It was probably for the best. The less stress for Jed, the better. *Then how can you possibly confront him with the scam?* her conscience nagged. *What will it do to him? Remember Patrick?*

Pressing her full lips together in determination, Megan tried not to think of the unhappy set of circumstances that had led to her succession as president of McKearn Investments. How she'd become president wasn't the issue; what she was going to do about the forthcoming scandal was. Jed had to know what was happening.

As she pulled into the circular drive of her parents' estate, she considered how she was going to break the news to Jed. Sooner or later he would find out about it, and she preferred to tell him about the scandal herself, somehow hoping to soften the blow. No doubt news of the scandal would leak to the press within the next couple of days. George Samples was the kind of man who would make sure his side of the story was told in screaming black and white.

And then there was Garrett Reaves. Megan knew him well enough to read the warnings in his dark, knowing eyes. If things didn't go Garrett's way, he would call his attorney and in a matter of days the story would be in all the local papers . . . including the *Denver Financial Times*. When the story hit the newsstands, McKearn Investments would be on the defensive.

Garrett's involvement, whether real or not, added an uncomfortable dimension to the problem. True, there was the personal angle; the man got to her, and she had trouble not believing the quiet dignity in his sharp hazel eyes. He set himself apart from the other clients involved in the scam.

But there was more to it than that. At least she hoped so. In all of the other accounts, the issue of involvement in the fraud was cut-and-dried. But with Reaves it was different; Megan hadn't convinced herself that he was a part of the swindle.

Uneasily she wondered if she were confusing her emotions with her business sense. Garrett Reaves still unnerved her—not as a wealthy account holder, but as a man.

With a disgusted sigh, Megan slid out of her Volvo. She attempted to relax as she strode determinedly up the front walk of the contemporary two-storied structure of cedar and glass that Jed and Anna McKearn had called home for the past ten years. Pushing the disturbing thoughts of Garrett out of her mind, Megan assumed an air of responsibility as she knocked once on the door before entering the house.

"I need to talk to Dad," Megan explained, after giving her mother an affectionate hug. Anna's smile faded slightly.

"About the business?"

Megan nodded, the expression on her soft features stern.

"Bad news," her mother guessed, running her fingers nervously along the single strand of pearls at her throat.

"Not the best."

Anna McKearn sighed. "I suppose he has to be

told. . . ." She shook her neatly styled red hair. "He's in the living room. "You know, it's almost as if he's been expecting you . . . strange."

Not so odd, Megan thought to herself. Jed McKearn had an uncanny sense of business and he could read his daughter like a book. Megan took a deep breath and strode into the living room to tell her father about Henry Silvas's report and the scam.

Jed McKearn was waiting for his only daughter. He looked out of place in the stark white room filled with bright contemporary furniture and vivid abstract *objets d'art*. Leaning against the sand-colored rocks of the fireplace, he listened patiently to Megan's story. His only indication of agitation was the nervous drumming of his fingers on the polished wood of his cane.

The stern-faced lecture she had been expecting didn't come. Megan had braced herself for one of Jed McKearn's explosive speeches when she told him about Henry Silvas's report. But Megan's father didn't chastise her or point out her flaws in handling the situation at McKearn Investments. He couldn't. He had hand-picked George Samples as a promising young broker from a competing brokerage.

Jed slowly shook his graying head and pursed his lips together in silent self-admonition. He looked older than his sixty-five years. His once robust appearance had paled, and his full face had hollowed noticeably.

Megan wondered if part of his ill health was directly the result of his concerns about his strong-willed daughter and her management of the business he had put his life into.

"You gave it your best shot, Meg. I can't expect anything more than that," he said, once she had briefly sketched out what had happened.

But he did expect more. Megan could read the undisguised disappointment in his sober expression. And the worst of it was that Jed McKearn blamed himself for what had happened. The guilt-ridden frown on his face gave his thoughts away.

"I should have listened when you came here a couple of months ago," he whispered. "I never thought George would get himself mixed up with something like this. Henry Silvas is sure of this thing, is he?"

"He's convinced that George was involved with someone at the *Times.*"

"How many accounts are involved?"

"Just a few. George brought most of them with him when he was hired."

"That's good," Jed remarked. "Those people probably knew what was happening."

Megan wondered how much she could tell her father and decided to make a clean breast of it before the papers distorted the story. "The only account that I'm worried about belongs to Garrett Reaves."

"Reaves was involved in this?" Jed's thin face tightened.

"It looks that way."

Jed nodded mutely. "Then you'd better watch your step."

Megan folded her arms over her chest and eyed her father warily. "You don't trust him?"

"I don't think the man is dishonest, if that's what

you mean," Jed said thoughtfully. "But he has a reputation of doing things his own way." Jed's dark eyes clouded in thought. "He got into a little trouble when he first bought out the shareholders of Mountain Chemical eight years ago. Don't you remember?"

"No," Megan whispered. "Eight years ago I was at Stanford and I wasn't too interested in what was going on here."

Jed's bushy gray brows pulled together. "That's right. Patrick was with me then . . ." His voice faded and he looked away from the pain in Megan's eyes.

"Reaves managed to be part of that, too," he muttered as if to himself. Lowering his gaunt body into a bright plum-colored chair, Jed leaned on the wooden cane and attempted a thin smile. "What do you plan to do now?" he asked quietly. A look of resigned defeat crossed his eyes and he bowed his shoulders. Megan knew that she had let him down— just as she had in the past.

Megan drew in a ragged breath as she settled onto the couch across from him. "Wait until I hear from Ted Benson and see what the SEC plans to do. Tonight I meet with Reaves and tomorrow with the board."

"To tell them about the swindle?"

"For starters." Megan's eyes were kind when they held her father's watery stare.

"Something else?"

"Yes, Dad, there is. I'm going to tender my resignation unless the board agrees that I have full control of what happens in the brokerage. I don't want to have to get your approval before I act. It's time-consuming and awkward. Right now, I'll have to act and react very quickly." She noticed the hint of regret in his eyes. "I hope that you'll back me up on this one."

Jed cracked a sincere smile and winked at her. "You've got it. Should have been that way from the start."

Megan felt as if a ton of bricks had been lifted from her shoulders. "I just hope the SEC doesn't shut me down."

Jed's head snapped upward and a trace of the old fire returned to his tired eyes. "Do you think they will?"

Shaking her head, Megan met her father's hardened gaze. "I don't think so, and both Henry Silvas and Ted Benson agree with me." She leaned back into the soft cushions. "Henry seems to think that they'll continue with the investigation and subpoena records from the company as well as from the newspaper involved."

"We can't afford a scandal."

Megan nodded her agreement. "Fortunately, we caught George before he did too much damage. It could have been worse."

"I suppose so," her father replied as if he didn't believe a word of it.

"Of course it could," Anna McKearn stated as she entered the room, she had heard a portion of the conversation. After setting a tray of iced tea on the small table separating father from daughter, she handed Megan a glass and caught her daughter's eye in a warning glance that begged Megan to be careful. Silently Anna reminded Megan once again of Jed's failing health. "Can't you stay for dinner?" the older woman asked, hoping to change the course of the conversation.

"I'd love to, Mom, but not tonight," Megan replied with a genuine smile.

"Business again?"

Megan took a sip of the cool amber liquid. She nodded at her mother's question. "I was just telling Dad about it. It looks like we have a problem."

"A sizable one, I gather," Anna mused.

"Nothing I can't handle," Megan replied evasively. Anna McKearn had never shown any interest in the business, and she couldn't understand Megan's fascination with the investment world. "I just wanted Dad to be prepared."

"For what?" Anna's blue eyes roved from Megan to Jed and back again before narrowing suspiciously. "What's going on?"

"It looks like one of the brokers is involved in some sort of swindle," Megan explained. "Several accounts are involved."

"And you wanted to tell us before the story got out," Anna surmised with a sad smile.

"McKearn Investments might be in for a little bad press," Megan admitted.

"Well, I guess we'll just have to weather it, won't we?" Megan's mother responded before casting a worried glance at her husband. "We have before."

"But it never gets any easier," Megan thought aloud as she got up from the couch and kissed her mother on the cheek. "I'll call you later," she whispered, cocking her head in the direction of her father. "Take care of him, will you?"

"You're the one who needs looking after," Jed interrupted grimly. "It's not going to be a picnic fighting with the SEC or Garrett Reaves."

"Aren't they both supposed to be on my side?"

"Time will tell," Jed whispered solemnly.

The clock chimed the quarter hour as Garrett made a mental wager with himself. What were the odds of Megan McKearn's knocking on his door tonight . . . after three years? And if she did make it—would she do as she had threatened and drag her attorney along with her? Deciding that the chances of Megan's showing up at all were slim, he scowled into the bottom of his empty glass.

It would be a cold day in hell before Megan returned to the rustic comfort of his mountain retreat. And yet he hoped to see her again. Garrett walked across the room and pulled out an unopened bottle of scotch. He frowned at the label, shrugged and splashed some of the liquor into his glass.

After taking a long swallow of the warm scotch, he kicked off his shoes, bent over the dry wood stacked on the hearth and tossed a couple of pieces of pine onto the fire. The smoldering embers ignited with a crackle against the pitchy wood and scented the air with the warm smell of burning pine.

Garrett's sharp eyes wandered to the window. It was already dark and Megan was a good fifteen minutes late. But that was to be expected, he tried to convince himself. The drive from Denver took over an hour in good weather. Rain pelted the windows and blurred his vision. The temperature was near freezing, and he wondered if the heavy drizzle would turn to snow before morning. Worried thoughts suddenly crowded his weary mind.

Once again he hazarded a glance at the clock. Eight-twenty. Could she have gotten lost—or worse? Weather conditions would make driving difficult. He tried to push away the unwelcome worry by concentrating on the matters at hand. If Megan McKearn didn't show up, he'd call his attorney and blow the story wide open. Either she played by his rules, or he took things into his own hands.

The winsome president of McKearn Investments was between the proverbial rock and a hard place. Garrett promised himself that he would battle with Megan . . . this time. The thought should have given him some glimmer of satisfaction. Strangely, it didn't.

If the contest between himself and Megan were so simple, why did he feel a nagging twinge of conscience when he remembered her sitting at the desk, her head in her palms, slim shoulders slumped in defeat, wild, coppery hair framing a worried face, tears gathering in her mysterious eyes?

Unable to answer the disturbing question, he lowered himself onto his favorite couch. He groaned when he stretched his long frame onto the worn leather cushions. The hours he had spent in a cramped position on the airplane were beginning to take their toll on him. His tired muscles were beginning to ache, and the strain of the long day hadn't been completely relieved by a hot shower. And now he was concerned for Megan's safety. Where was she?

Carefully balancing his drink on his abdomen,

Garrett stared at the exposed beams of the ceiling. Eerie shadows cast from the fire shifted silently throughout the room. Just for a moment, he closed his eyes and tried to relax. He wanted to think through the dilemma of Megan McKearn and the problem at hand, but other images assailed him. He remembered lying on this same couch with her, feeling the warm texture of her skin pressed intimately against him, tasting the salt of her sweat trickling seductively between her gorgeous breasts. . . . Just at the thought of her, he groaned and forced his thoughts away from the subtle allure in her intelligent eyes.

The woman aroused feelings within him that he had hoped were buried far too deep to resurface, and he wondered if insisting she come here had been an incredible miscalculation. There was still something seductive and enticing about her, something he couldn't name and didn't like to consider. He knew instinctively that he should avoid the sensual promises of her dove gray eyes.

Yet he was the one who had demanded that she come here, to the remote seclusion of the mountains. "You're a damn fool," he softly swore before stretching his fingers and pushing them recklessly through his dark hair. "Even if she tried, she'd have a hell of a time remembering how to find this place."

His home was located northeast of Boulder in the rugged foothills of the Rocky Mountains. Sometimes the commute to Denver was tedious, but he had decided long ago that his privacy was well worth the price of an extra hour or two on the road.

After draining the remainder of his scotch, he

refocused his eyes to stare through the window and into the night. In the distance he noticed pale beams from the headlights of a car winding through the thick stands of pine trees surrounding his estate. He heaved a sigh of relief.

Then his square jaw hardened and a gleam of satisfaction flickered triumphantly in his eyes. Hoisting his empty glass toward the window, he saluted her with a mock toast.

"Congratulations, Ms. McKearn. You've got more guts than I gave you credit for."

Megan squinted into the darkness and her fingers tightened over the cold steering wheel. She was already late, and the narrow road with its sharp curves was difficult to follow. Rain ran down the windshield despite the tireless effort of the wipers to slap it aside.

A newscast from the radio reminded her of the time, and she grimaced as she turned the radio off and rounded the final bend in the road.

He was expecting her. Half a dozen floodlights illuminated the immense house hidden in the stately pines. Warm lamp glow from the interior of the house spilled through the windows to diffuse into the dark night.

She stopped the car and killed the engine as she reached the garage. Hiking her raincoat around her neck, Megan grabbed her briefcase and, after only a moment's hesitation, opened the car door. The rain had softened to a gentle mist. With renewed determination Megan hurried up the walk toward the gracious Tudor manor. Hardly a mountain cabin.

The house was constructed of gray stone and heavy dark timbers. It rose three stories from the knoll on which it stood, and the deep pitch of the roof was angled with several intricate dormers. Megan remembered it all too well.

After rapping soundly on the solid oak door, Megan waited and forced her wandering thoughts away from the troubling past. Within moments the door was opened and she was staring into the intense hazel eyes of Garrett Reaves. The scrutiny of his gaze was as seductive as it had been on the night she first met him.

Tonight Garrett was dressed casually in gray cords and an ivory sweater. The sleeves were pushed over his forearms, revealing tanned skin stretched over taut, corded muscles. An expectant smile played on his lips.

"You made it." He sounded relieved.

"I said I would. Sorry I'm late . . . I forgot that you lived halfway to Wyoming," she responded, her cheeks coloring slightly under his studious inspection.

"Not quite that far." His smile broadened into an appreciative grin that tempered the harsh angles of his face. He stepped out of the doorway, allowing enough room for her to pass. "Please come in." And then he added, "I take it Benson couldn't join you?"

"A little short notice, wouldn't you say? Most attorneys have busy schedules and better things to do than bow down to the demands of the opposition."

Instead of becoming incensed, Garrett smiled—a

deadly smile that could play havoc with her rational thought.

Brushing past him, she ignored the warmth of his grin and the familiarity it engendered. Megan reminded herself of the past and the pain and the fact that he was most likely involved in the current scam at the investment company.

She stood in the expansive foyer and eyed the opulent warmth of the interior. Soft light from a suspended brass fixture bathed the entry in a warm glow that reflected in the patina of the oak floors and the rosewood paneling on the walls. A staircase, complete with a hand-hewn wooden banister, climbed up the far wall before disappearing into the floor above. Tapestries in vibrant hues of royal blue and burgundy adorned the walls, and handwoven Persian rugs in the same rich colors were carefully placed on the floor.

Megan studied the expensive furnishings as she absently unbuttoned her coat. Nothing much had changed. When she returned her eyes to the man in the doorway, she discovered that he was staring at her, watching intently as she slowly slid the final button through the hole to remove the mauve raincoat.

Their gazes locked. For an instant, Megan's throat constricted. His knowing hazel eyes searched hers and made a silent promise that touched a feminine part of her soul. Megan was forced to look away from the unspoken invitation. *He's doing it to you again,* she warned, swallowing against the tightness in her chest.

"Let me take your coat," he suggested as she pulled her arms out of the sleeves. When he helped her remove the garment, his fingers brushed against the back of her neck. She tried to ignore the delicacy of his touch and the faint tremor of anticipation his fingers had inspired.

After hanging the coat over one of the curved spokes of an antique hall tree, Garrett turned toward a hallway branching from the foyer toward the rear of the house. "Would you like a drink?" he asked, leading her into the library she remembered all too well. Bookcases with glass doors filled the wall between the fireplace and the bay window.

"Some wine, if you have it," she replied, taking a seat in one of the chairs near the stone fireplace. She opened her briefcase to withdraw the documents concerning his account at McKearn Investments, then adjusted her reading glasses on her face. She was thankful to discuss business.

"Why don't you level with me, Megan, and tell me just exactly what's going on." He handed her a glass of chilled Chablis and leaned against the warm stones of the fireplace. Eyeing her speculatively over the rim of his glass, Garrett took a sip of his scotch.

She smiled faintly and set her wineglass on the small table near her chair. "I've known that something was wrong for quite a while," she replied.

"With my account?"

She shook her head, and the firelight caught in the raindrops still lingering in her hair. "No, I had no idea your account was involved. I just knew . . . had a feeling that something wasn't right."

"A feeling? This is all based on a *feeling?*" The

warmth on his face faded. The intimacy between them dissolved into the night.

"Of course not," Megan replied, her eyes meeting his frosty gaze steadily. "It started out as a feeling—something I really couldn't define—so I called an accountant for an unscheduled audit of all the books. Every account was studied."

"Including mine."

"Right."

"And how many accounts turned out to be . . . suspect?"

"There were several. Nine altogether."

"And the broker of record for all of the accounts just happened to be George Samples," Garrett surmised, frowning darkly into his drink. When she nodded, he let out a disgusted breath of air. "Okay, so what happened, exactly, to cause all of this commotion?"

Megan extracted photocopies of the clippings from the *Denver Financial Times* from her briefcase. She handed him the articles, along with a copy of his latest statement. He surveyed the documents warily, scanning the trades circled in red. The furrow on his forehead deepened. "I don't understand . . . ," he murmured, but his voice trailed off as he raised his eyes to meet hers. "The trades were made before the articles were printed," he guessed, checking the dates on the clippings against the statement.

"And you didn't know about it?" Her eyebrows lifted dubiously over the frames of her glasses.

"No."

"But *you* have control over your account. All of those trades were authorized by you."

"Of course they were." His fingers rubbed the tension gathering in the back of his neck as he tried to come up with a logical explanation.

"How do you explain that?"

"It's simple. Samples would call me with an investment suggestion. If I agreed with his line of thinking, I'd tell him to go ahead with the trade."

"But you didn't know where his foresight in the market was coming from?"

Hazel eyes drilled into hers, and the features on his face became stern. "Did *you?*" When she didn't immediately respond, he crossed the small space separating them and leaned over her chair, boldly pushing his face near hers. "I assumed that George Samples was a sharp broker. Your father seemed to think that he was, and everything he did for me worked to my advantage."

He was so close to her that his warm breath, laced with the scent of scotch, touched her face. "It seems to me, Megan, that I should be the one asking the questions here, not you. If my account was inappropriately used, it was because I trusted you—or at least your father—and the integrity of McKearn Investments. Jed was always as good as his word, and his advice had been sound in the past. Why would I question his judgment? As for George Samples, the bastard proved himself to me."

"By making money for you illegally."

"*I* didn't know that." His thick brows blunted. "You see, I was under the impression that anyone working for McKearn Investments was honest and hardworking. You know, full of good old American integrity."

Megan shifted uneasily in the chair and took a sip of the cool Chablis to wet her suddenly dry throat. All of Garrett's insinuations were vocalizations of her own fears. Pensively twirling the long stem of the glass, she thought aloud, "Generally, they are—"

"Except for Samples," he viciously reminded her. "If anyone should have known what he was doing, it was *you*. You're running the investment company. George Samples worked for you." Garrett seemed to be warming to his subject. His eyes narrowed menacingly. "And as far as profiting from his trades, how about McKearn Investments? Certainly its reputation wasn't hurt by Samples's underhanded deals. He made you look good—damn good." Garrett straightened, putting some distance between his lean frame and hers. His dark eyes never left her face and continued to drive his point home.

"Until now," she retorted. "McKearn Investments is left holding the bag because of one man and his greed."

"You should have been on top of this, Ms. McKearn," Garrett charged. "From day one."

She couldn't argue with him, nor would she admit that part of her problem stemmed from listening to her father's advice. Any excuse would sound as flimsy as it was. The bottom line was that Megan McKearn was responsible for what had transpired while she was calling the shots. "Arguing about it won't solve the problem."

"But *you* can, at least as far as I'm concerned." He placed a foot on the raised hearth and leaned his elbow on his bent knee. His sweater stretched across the broad muscles of his back.

She was instantly wary. "How?"

"By removing my account and my name from suspicion. Come on, Megan, you know me well enough to realize that I had no part in this. What George Samples did has no reflection on me."

"Except for the trade involving Reaves Chemical," Megan replied, her gray eyes never wavering.

"What trade?"

"Look on your April statement." He shuffled the papers until he came to the page in question. His eyes scanned the figures as Megan continued to speak. "On April tenth, you asked George to sell short on your own company's stock. Was that his idea?"

"There shouldn't have been any problem. He suggested it. I filed all the appropriate papers—" A muscle tightened in the corner of his jaw, and his eyes took on a deadly gleam.

Megan's heart was pounding erratically. What she was about to suggest was difficult, and her throat became dry with dread. "Of course you did, but that doesn't matter. What's important is the fact that you made nearly a hundred thousand dollars on that trade alone."

"Is that a crime, Ms. McKearn?" he asked, his voice dangerously low, his hazel eyes threatening.

"I don't know," she admitted. "That's for the SEC to determine. . . ." Her voice trailed off, and she wondered if she'd given too much of herself away.

"There's more, isn't there?" he guessed, inexplicably reading the hesitation in her gaze. "It's more than that one trade."

"You profited from several of the transactions."

"Of course I did!" he snapped back, throwing his arms up in disgust. "I haven't a clue why Samples decided to use my account—it doesn't make any sense. Why involve me?" His bewilderment appeared sincere, and every muscle in his whip-lean body tensed.

Megan watched his sure movements. Were they well rehearsed, or was he really as disgusted as he seemed? Her wide eyes scrutinized his chiseled features, searching for the smallest trace of emotion that might give his thoughts away.

Garrett frowned darkly as he tossed another piece of wood onto the fire and jabbed at it with a piece of kindling. His cords stretched over his tightly muscled thighs and buttocks, and Megan forced her attention back to the harsh planes of his masculine face.

Dusting his hands on his pants, Garrett straightened before turning to face her again.

"You have no idea why George would involve you?" she asked, running a tense finger over the rim of her wineglass.

"No. Unless it wasn't George at all, but his boss." His lips drew into a thin, tight line and his dark gaze pierced into hers.

"Meaning me?"

"Right—a personal vendetta."

Megan's gray eyes flared with indignation. "No matter what happened between us, Garrett," she whispered with ironclad determination, "I would never sabotage your account."

"Revenge is supposed to be sweet," he ventured, purposely goading her.

"You would know."

He grimaced. "You swore that you hated me," he reminded her, and visions of that wild night filled with heated passion and dark despair raced through her head.

"Why would I have waited so long?"

"Maybe because you never had the opportunity before."

"I don't think there's a reason to dignify your insinuations with an answer! If you'll excuse me . . ." She stood and straightened her shoulders, intent on leaving him to his ridiculous hypotheses.

Garrett studied her a moment and seemed convinced by her outburst. "Relax, Megan . . . I'm sorry. I just had to be sure that this wasn't your way of getting even."

"It isn't," she replied coldly.

"Then my guess is that good old George did it for protection."

"Protection?" Megan's interest was piqued. She set her unfinished glass of wine on the table and removed her reading glasses. "What do you mean?"

"It's just a guess, Megan, but the only plausible explanation is that George was hedging his bets. He must have known that he might get caught, and he was hoping that I might be able to bail him out."

"How?" Megan settled back into her chair, her eyes never leaving the rigid contours of Garrett's face.

Garrett shrugged indifferently. "I've got the best lawyers in town working for me. I also have some influence in Denver—which George must have known wouldn't hurt his cause. Samples is shrewd.

He must have figured that I'd fight this thing with everything I've got." He read the disbelief in her eyes. The corner of his mouth twisted downward. "I said it was only a guess."

"There might be another reason," she ventured.

His eyebrows lifted, silently inviting her to continue.

"Maybe the profitable trades were a way of repaying a favor."

"A favor? To me? What are you getting at?" The anger he had restrained started to simmer as he began to understand her convoluted line of reasoning. In the long seconds that followed, only the crackle of the fire disturbed the silence.

"I just wondered if you knew that you weren't the only one who made money selling short on Reaves Chemical. Some of George's other accounts earned a substantial amount of cash by following your example." Her voice was controlled but her stomach was twisting in painful knots. She had come a hairsbreadth from accusing Garrett of leaking confidential information about Reaves Chemical for profit.

The insinuation hit its mark. Garrett's skin tightened over his cheekbones, and he had to force himself to maintain a modicum of control over his seething anger. "You're grasping at straws, Megan. You and that investment company of yours are in a tight spot and you're looking for a scapegoat."

"We don't need one," she interjected with more authority than she felt. "George Samples took care of that."

"And you're willing to hang me along with him?"

"I think you've hung yourself."

"This is a frame-up, isn't it?" He shook his dark head and snorted disdainfully. "God, Megan, I would have expected more from you than some cheap swindle—"

"Look, I'm not about to hang anyone. Not you—or George Samples, for that matter," Megan interjected. Why was it suddenly so important that he understand her? "I'm just trying to clear all this up so that I can talk to Ted Benson or the SEC and give them some answers."

"So that you don't look like a fool!"

Megan sighed and shook her head. "So that I can prevent these mistakes from being repeated. And, if you'll remember, I came here because you asked me to."

He stared into the honesty in her wide gray eyes. The same vulnerability that he had witnessed so many times in the past was present in her gaze. He had seen it fleetingly this afternoon, and it was evident now as well. It was a softness she tried to hide, but it wouldn't leave him alone.

Absurdly, he wondered what it would be like to kiss her eyelids and try to erase the pain she quietly bore. The pain he had inadvertently caused years ago.

"So where does that leave us, Megan?" he asked.

"With a problem. A very big problem."

Chapter Four

Leaning his shoulder against the mantel, Garrett thoughtfully ran his thumb along his jaw as he stared at Megan with undisguised interest.

"What you meant to say was that McKearn Investments has a problem," he speculated. Moving his eyes from the gentle contours of her face, he looked through the window and squinted into the darkness. Before she could reply, he continued. "And you don't really know how to handle it."

Megan bristled. "I think I've done all right so far—"

"But the going hasn't got tough yet. Just wait till the press gets a hold of this. They're going to have a field day," he predicted. "And all at the expense of McKearn Investments."

"Your name will come up."

He lifted his shoulders and returned his intense

gaze to her worried face. Her gray eyes had clouded
with uncertainty, and he pressed his point home.
"I'm used to it. Chemical companies are always
under the gun because of new products. No matter
how many times you test a new drug, and despite
approval from the FDA, there's always a chance that
somewhere, with the right combination of other
stimuli, something might go wrong. But with you it's
different," he guessed, noting the nervous manner in
which her fingers slid back and forth on the loosely
woven fabric of the chair.

"A scandal is never easy," she replied, meeting
his discomforting stare.

"Especially when it falls so quickly on the heels of
another one."

Her spine stiffened and the color drained from her
face. Her eyes, when they returned to his, were wide
and shadowed in silent agony. "You should know,"
she whispered, hiding a trace of bitterness.

Unforgiving eyes drilled into hers. "You still
blame me for Patrick's death, don't you?" he
charged.

"What happened to my brother has nothing to do
with the reason I came here."

"The hell it doesn't."

Her fingers were trembling, and she was forced to
press them into her palms to quiet the storm of
emotions raging silently within her. Tears, hot with
betrayal, stung her eyes.

"But that's what this is all about," he insisted.
"The scandal involving your brother taught you a
lesson. You're trying to find a way to take the heat
off of yourself and your family." Dark eyes chal-

lenged her to disagree as he crossed the small distance separating them.

Megan rose from the chair. Her chin inched upward in silent defiance. "I came here tonight to reason with you."

"You came because you didn't have much of a choice."

"I was hoping that we could talk this out—"

"You were looking for someone to blame."

Her face paled under his vicious accusations, but she stood her ground. "I think I should leave," she said, reaching for her glasses and quickly putting them into her purse. Indicating the loose stack of papers lying on the table with a tired wave of her hand, she turned toward the door. "You can keep those. I have other copies."

She reached for her briefcase, but Garrett's hand restrained her. Warm fingers closed over the bend in her arm. "This is always your answer, isn't it? Running from the truth."

"I'm not running from anything—"

His fingers tightened. "Knock it off, Megan. I know you. Remember? I was there the night Patrick was killed. You ran that night, too. Who was it you couldn't face? Me? Or yourself?"

The lump in her throat made it difficult to speak. She closed her eyes against the haunting memories of the dark night Patrick was killed. Guilt, like a heavy black shroud, settled on her slim shoulders. They sagged from the burden. "This . . . this isn't getting us anywhere." She straightened her spine, aware of his fingers still pressing warmly through the silken fabric of her blouse.

"I don't know about that."

She looked down disdainfully at the hand on her arm. "If you think you can goad me into saying something I'll regret later, you'd better forget it. And bringing up the past won't help. Ted Benson—"

"Leave him out of this. What's happening here is between you and me. Period. We don't need lawyers, accountants *or* the SEC to clutter things up."

"I think I'd better go . . ."

The grip on her arm tightened. "I'm only trying to uncover the truth."

Her lips curved into a disbelieving smile. "And that's why I came here—"

"Is it?" His eyes threw dark challenge in her face. Erotically, they probed into the most secret part of her mind.

"I thought I owed you the benefit of the doubt. I'm sorry I wasted your time."

"You don't *owe* me anything, lady. You came here because you thought you might be able to talk me out of a potential lawsuit."

"I hoped that you would be reasonable." The arch of her brow indicated she now realized the folly of such a hope.

"Damn it, woman, I'm trying . . ." With his free hand he rubbed the back of his neck, as if in that single action he could relieve the tension of the long day. He closed his eyes for a fraction of a second and squeezed them tight.

The fingers coiled possessively over her elbow didn't relax. She tried to withdraw her arm. "I think I'd better go . . ."

"Megan," he whispered gently as his eyes opened.

Her name lingered in the warmth of the room and brought back the memories of yesterday. Firelight and shadows made his face appear strained, and the regret in his eyes seemed sincere. "Let's not argue." Silently his eyebrows lifted as if to encourage an intimacy she had hoped to avoid.

Megan swallowed against the dryness settling in the back of her throat as his fingers moved seductively up her arm. "Wait. Look, I think we should stick to the issue at hand. Bringing up what happened to my brother is beside the point." She felt his quiet fury in the grip on her arm.

"But that's why you're here, Megan. Face it. You and I both know that you came here tonight because I threatened you with a lawsuit. That coupled with the scandal could cripple McKearn Investments. You're afraid that McKearn Investments can't weather another scandal. Not after all the rumors and speculation about Patrick's death."

"Do you really think you have that much influence—?"

"I know I do." His dark eyes hardened.

Megan moistened her lips and shook her head. "I think the corporation can stand the adverse publicity—"

"But can you—or your family?" he demanded, roughly shaking her imprisoned arm. "How do you think your father is going to react to another public disgrace? How do you think it will affect his health?"

The anger that had been simmering quietly within her suddenly exploded. Her voice shook. "You really can be a bastard, can't you?"

"Only when I have to be." His hard features

softened as he gazed into her furious gaze. "You've pushed me into a corner, Megan, and I'm trying to claw my way out. This is nothing personal—"

"Nothing personal!" She couldn't mask her disbelief. "How can you stand there and say that your repeated attacks against my family aren't personal, for God's sake! First you bring up my brother's death, and now my dad's health. What are you trying to do—browbeat me into submission? Do you expect me to cower from all your vague threats?" Her gray eyes moved upward in cool appraisal. "I'm not as weak as I used to be."

"I think you're a lot of things, Megan. But weak? Never. I'm just trying to make you understand my position."

"Which is?"

"That I'm innocent, damn it!"

"Then why the scare tactics?" She tried to step away from him, to put some distance between his anger and hers, to separate the intimacy of their bodies. He placed his free hand on her shoulder, as if by physically touching her he could communicate his feelings.

"I think you should know what you're up against," he whispered ominously. His eyes darkened seductively as he stared down at her upturned face.

"Meaning you—your money, your lawyers, your *power*." Her breath caught in her throat as she watched his anger disappear, to be replaced by something infinitely more dangerous.

"I won't let my name be dragged through the

mud. Nor will I sit idle while your auditor and the SEC set out to destroy me. I had no part in George Samples's scheme, and I'll do everything in my power to prove it!"

"Then you *are* threatening me—"

"No. I'm just telling you what's going to happen so that you can be prepared." He hesitated a moment, as if unsure of his words. "You have to believe one thing, Megan," he whispered, gazing deeply into her eyes.

Her pulse was racing wildly at the intimacy of his tone, but she managed to raise one eyebrow to encourage him to continue.

"I would never . . . never do anything to hurt you."

He seemed so honest, and yet all she had to do was remember the past to see through his lies. "Unless you were forced into it."

He winced as if she had stabbed him. His grip on her shoulders tightened. Slowly, he drew her body to his until she could feel the hard contour of his chest pressed against her breasts. His breath, laced with the scent of scotch, fanned her cheeks. She felt the heat of his desire in his touch and noticed the smoldering passion in his searching gaze.

Her heart was pounding erratically in her chest, and the blood rushed through her veins in unwanted, betraying desire.

I can't want this man, she told herself vainly; *not after what he did to me!* His head lowered and his lips hovered expectantly over hers.

Garrett isn't trustworthy, she cautioned herself.

He would do anything to make me believe him. She knew it in her heart, and yet she couldn't resist the bittersweet temptation of his caress.

His lips touched hers lightly . . . softly enticing a response from her with his gentle kiss. She tried not to respond; her arms reached upward in defense and her hands pressed against his chest to push away from him, but her efforts were futile. Her fingers, instead of forestalling the attack, moved gently against the knit of his sweater and felt the lean, rock-hard muscles of his chest. Memories, long silent and aching with torment, filled her mind. It seemed like only yesterday when he had last held her.

He groaned and his strong fingers splayed against the small of her back, silently urging her to press against him. Hard, unyielding thighs touched hers. His breathing was as rough as her own. His lips continued to mold against hers, becoming more bold with each bittersweet second that passed. His tongue touched her lips, daring to part her mouth and slide against the polish of her teeth before insistently slipping into the warm invitation of her mouth.

Megan was aware that her knees were weakening and that her arms had wound around Garrett's neck. She knew that she was playing the part of the fool, but she couldn't resist the seductive magic of his touch. Closing her eyes against the painful thought, she sighed and gave in to the intimacy of the night. They were alone, separated from the world, and all she could consider was the warmth of his embrace.

Strong arms secured her against him, catching her

protectively as the weight of his body pressed her urgently but gently to the carpeted floor.

The hands that held her moved slowly up her back to the tight knot of hair at the base of her head. Gently cradling her head as he kissed her, Garrett let his fingers twine in the thickly coiled braid before slowly withdrawing the pins holding the sleek knot in place. Her hair tumbled in soft curls to rest in seductive disarray at her shoulders. Amber light from the fire caught in the burnished strands, gilding her hair with fiery highlights.

"You're beautiful," he murmured against the gentle curve of her throat. His hands loosened the first button of her blouse and the soft silken fabric parted. He kissed the exposed white skin, and Megan shuddered as a chill of reality ran through her.

It would be so easy to fall in love with him again.

"No," she whispered faintly, her protest feeble.

Another button came free of its bond.

"Please . . . Garrett."

His head dipped lower and his wet lips made a dewy impression against the delicate curve of her collarbone.

The third button slid out of its restraint.

Megan tried to clear her mind, attempted to cool her body from the warm inspiration of his touch. The cool night air caressed her skin, and his lips brushed gently in the hollow between her breasts.

"I can't," she whispered. "Garrett, please, this is wrong."

His hands stopped their gentle exploration and he

looked up to stare into her eyes. "It's never been wrong with you," he persisted, his voice rough.

"I don't love you, Garrett," she said, her tongue nearly tripping on the lie. "Maybe I never did." A challenge, bright with frustration, burned in his gaze. "I . . . I should never have let this happen," she admitted, trying to soothe the pain of rejection. Shaking her head, she fought against the unwanted tears burning in her throat. "I had no intention . . ."

"Neither did I." She watched him will back the rising tide of passion that had washed over him.

"I'm sorry . . ."

"Megan . . . ," he whispered, reaching upward and softly touching her hair. "There's no need to apologize."

Her voice caught at the tenderness of the gesture, and the tears began to pool in her eyes. "I didn't mean to let things go so far."

"Shhh . . . it's okay." He took her into his arms and softly kissed her forehead.

"I've got to go." Quickly she began to rebutton her blouse. *How had she let things get so out of hand? Was she really still so susceptible to him? Why was it so easy to forget the pain of the past? Garrett's betrayal?* She extracted herself from his embrace and reached for her purse.

"You don't believe me," he guessed as his lips pulled into an incredulous frown. "After everything we've been through, you still think I had something to do with this scam."

She shook her head and the firelight played in the coppery strands of her hair. "I hope you didn't," she

whispered fervently. "I hope to God you're innocent."

His dark eyes pierced her soul. "Trust me."

"Oh, Garrett, if it were only that easy," she
whispered, holding his gaze.

He reached forward and traced her chin with his
finger. "It's as easy as you make it. Stay with me
tonight . . ."

She smiled wistfully. His offer was more tempting
than she would like to admit. "I can't. You know
that. It would only make things more difficult."

"You've never forgiven me, have you?"

"Do you blame me? You *lied* to me." She forced
back the uncomfortable lump in her throat, and her
eyes narrowed to glinting slits of silvery suspicion.
"You were engaged to Lana. All the time that we
were together."

"That's not the way it was," he protested, his dark
brows blunting.

"I'm not used to being 'the other woman.' It's a
role I try to avoid." She pulled herself to her feet,
but he was beside her in an instant, his hazel eyes
glowering with indignation. As she attempted to
walk out of the room, he placed his hands possessively on her shoulders and forced her to turn and
face him.

"Believe me, Megan, I never thought of you as
anything but the only woman in my life."

For a moment she was tempted to believe the pain
in his eyes. It would be so easy to trust him and fall
victim to his seduction all over again.

But the truth came back to her in a blinding flash.

All too vividly, Megan remembered the yellowed article that Patrick had silently handed to her only hours before his death. A picture of Garrett, with his arms draped lovingly over Lana Tremaine's shoulders, had accompanied the announcement of Garrett's engagement to the attractive blond heiress.

She closed her eyes and stepped away from him. "It doesn't matter . . . not anymore. I've said what I had to say to you. Anything else should be handled through my attorney." She whirled on her heel and headed for the door.

"Megan."

She hesitated only slightly but kept walking. In the foyer, she reached for her coat but didn't bother to put it on. She had to get away. Away from the house. Away from the lies. Away from Garrett.

She heard his footsteps as he pursued her. He caught up with her just as she reached for the handle of the door. She turned the knob and tugged. The door opened a crack before Garrett's flat hand pressed against the smooth wood and pushed it shut.

"You've got to believe that I had no part in this, Meg."

Her slim shoulders sagged. "Why?"

"Because I'm innocent, damn it!"

"So you've been saying."

"I thought that, in this country, one was still innocent until proven guilty."

"The evidence—"

"Circumstantial."

"But convincing."

His muscles tensed and he let his hand fall away

from the door. "I'm going to fight this thing with whatever it takes."

"Good night, Garrett." Without a backward glance, she pulled open the door and disappeared into the night.

Garrett waited until the car engine started, the headlights illuminated the rain-drenched night and Megan drove quickly away from his home. As he heard her tires squeal against the wet pavement, his concern for her resurfaced. "Be careful," he whispered in the direction of the disappearing vehicle.

A few moments later, he closed the door and strode back into the den, silently leveling an oath at the disturbing set of circumstances that had brought her so decidedly back into his life.

He grabbed the receiver of the phone and punched out the private number of Ron Thurston. One of Thurston's teenaged kids answered the phone, and Garrett had to wait. He scowled into the fire while his fingers drummed restlessly on the scarred maple desk.

"Hello?"

"Ron? Garrett Reaves."

"What the devil?" the surprised attorney asked. "For heaven's sake, Reaves, why are you calling me at this hour?"

"I didn't mean to call you so late—"

"Don't worry about it. Jason was beating the pants off me at one of those damned video games." Ron Thurston chuckled at the thought of his son whipping him. "What's up?"

"It looks like I might be in a little trouble."

Instantly the attorney sobered. "The McKearn Investment scam," Thurston guessed. This wasn't the first of Garrett's calls. Nor would it be the last.

"That's right."

"You still think you're being framed?"

Garrett rubbed the tension from the back of his neck with his free hand. "Sure of it."

"By whom?"

Megan's name hovered on the tip of his tongue. She was the logical choice. The woman with the means and the motive. By all rights, she should hate anything associated with Garrett Reaves. But her response tonight had surprised him. More than once he had caught a trace of longing in her silvery eyes. "I'm not sure," Garrett hedged, realizing that he had created a lag in the conversation. "But I'd start with George Samples."

"Did he have it in for you?"

"I don't think so—anyway, I couldn't begin to guess why."

There was a pause on the other end of the line. Garrett suspected that Ron, who's interest was aroused, was taking quick notes on his ever-present legal pad. "Anyone else?"

Garrett hedged. "I doubt it. But you might check into all the members of the McKearn family."

"Jed and his daughter?"

Taking in a sharp breath of air, Garrett replied. "Yes."

"Okay. Got it. You planning to file against McKearn Investments?"

"You tell me."

"I will. After I do some checking—tomorrow."

"Thanks, Ron."

"Later."

When Garrett hung up, the warm sense of vengeful satisfaction he had hoped to find was sadly missing. He walked over to the bar, contemplating another drink, and kicked at an imaginary adversary before splashing three fingers of scotch into his glass.

As he sat on the hearth, cradling the warm liquor in both of his hands, his thoughts centered on Megan. It had been a mistake to get involved with her three years ago. He had known it at the time. And it was an even bigger mistake to get involved with her now, when there was so much at stake. But he couldn't help himself. Whenever he thought about her, his head began to throb and the desire in his loins caught fire. It had never been that way with any other woman. Even Lana. At the thought of his ex-wife, Garrett frowned in disgust and swallowed the remainder of his drink.

Megan shuddered as if with a sudden chill, but her hands were sweaty where she gripped the steering wheel. "Don't let him get to you," she warned herself as she took a corner too quickly and the tires slid on the wet pavement.

Thoughts of Garrett and his erotic touch wouldn't leave her alone. She could still taste the hint of scotch on her lips where he had kissed her. "Don't be a fool," she whispered scathingly. "He only wants something from you—just like he did in the past."

Chapter Five

$\mathcal{T}$he board meeting the following day went reasonably well. Despite a poor night's sleep filled with dreams of making love to Garrett, Megan managed to pull herself together and face the curious members of the board with the news of the investment scam and potential scandal.

After the initial shock had worn off, each of the members had studied the photocopied statements and the evidence against George Samples. Megan explained her position, and with only a few minor grumbles, the board backed her up.

When she gave her ultimatum requesting complete authority without having to seek approval of her decisions from Jed, there was some dissent. However, Gordon Wells, a personal friend of Jed's, came to her defense and convinced the other board members that Megan's temporary position should be considered permanent.

"You can't expect her to operate with her hands tied, Marian," the rotund ex-banker had responded to Mrs. Chatwick's objections.

"But what about Jed?"

Gordon Wells's eyes were kind. "We all expected Jed to return, but . . . well, we have to face facts. Jed's health has been deteriorating for quite a while. We have an obligation to the stockholders to run this company as well as can be expected—with or without Jed."

"I explained everything to my father last night. He supports me in my decision," Megan stated, her gray eyes calm but determined. "Now I think we should concentrate on the problem at hand and how we're going to deal with it."

From that point on, there were no further objections. Ted Benson pointed out the legalities of the situation and explained that he had been in contact with the local office of the Securities and Exchange Commission.

After the board meeting, Megan had lunch with Ted Benson in a small bistro on the Sixteenth Street Mall. The restaurant was intimate and quiet. Business could be discussed without too much fear of being overheard.

The tables near the windows offered an interesting view of the pedestrians hurrying along the flagstone mall and rushing into the various shops, boutiques and eating establishments. Slow-moving shuttle buses ambled down the length of the mall, past white metal chairs and wood benches located on the flagstones.

Megan's lunch consisted of fresh shrimp salad, hot tea with lemon and a tense discussion with the attorney for McKearn Investments.

"I mentioned at the board meeting that I've been in contact with the SEC," Ted announced, his piercing blue eyes stone cold as he pushed aside his plate.

Megan felt her muscles tighten defensively. Had Ted or the SEC found incriminating evidence proving that Garrett had been involved? She sipped her tea and met Ted's cold gaze without hesitation. "And?"

"They were onto the scam. Had it monitored by one of their computer systems."

Megan nodded. She had expected as much. George Samples was a fool to think that he could get away with so obvious a swindle. "What did they say?"

"Not much. Obviously, the investigation is still in progress."

"Do they want to talk to me?"

Ted shook his head of thick white hair and frowned before taking a long swallow of his tea. Bushy dark brows guarded his intense eyes. "So far, they haven't wanted to speak to anyone."

"Isn't that odd?"

"I don't think so. They're probably just getting all the facts."

"What about the accounts involved?"

Ted shrugged his broad shoulders, withdrew a cigarette and lit it. "We'll just have to sit tight and see what the SEC comes up with. So will the account holders," he decided as he inhaled deeply on the cigarette. "We don't have much choice in the matter. For now, it's business as usual."

"Easy for you to say," Megan observed with a wry smile.

"Take it easy, Meg. *You* haven't done anything illegal."

"Tell that to the SEC."

"I did."

Megan couldn't help thinking about Garrett. Was he involved in the swindle up to his seductive hazel eyes, or was he an innocent victim of George Samples's scam?

"Something wrong?" Ted asked, assuming a concern that was far from fatherly.

Megan managed a tight smile. "You mean something *else?*"

"You're a million miles away." He stubbed out his cigarette as a waiter discreetly left the bill on the table.

"I was just wondering how many of George's accounts were in this with him."

"All of them," the attorney said without equivocation. "That is, all of the accounts that Henry Silvas dug up." The attorney smiled broadly. "Are you sure I can't get you a drink?"

Megan shook her head and refused to be deterred from the subject. "Even Garrett Reaves's account?" Megan questioned, watching Ted's reaction.

Ted sighed audibly. For two years he'd been interested in Megan, but he could never lure their conversation away from business. "Even Reaves. He has a reputation for stepping on anyone he has to in order to make a buck. Seems to me that this sort of thing would be right up his alley." He left some bills on the table, stood and thereby dismissed the subject.

Megan wasn't put off. "But why? Why would a man of his stature take such a risk?"

"Money."

"Reaves has money."

"Okay then, *more* money. No one ever has enough." He carefully retrieved Megan's raincoat and helped her on with it. "That's what keeps lawyers like me in Porsches. Greed."

"You think Garrett Reaves is greedy?"

Ted held the door open for her and smiled. "No, I think people in general are greedy. Reaves is no different."

"Wanting to make some money and going about it illegally are two different things."

Ted Benson shrugged. "Maybe." They walked, heads bent against an icy wind, toward the Jefferson Tower and the offices of McKearn Investments. "But men have gone to almost any lengths to make money or keep their business afloat."

"Reaves Chemical seems to be solid," Megan countered.

"But he's expanding—maybe more rapidly than he should. There's the plant in Japan—another under consideration in Brazil. All that takes money." He noticed the look of wariness in Megan's eyes and changed tactics. "Look, in all fairness to Reaves, I suppose it's possible that he's not involved in the swindle."

"But unlikely?"

Ted squinted his steely blue eyes over his hawkish nose. "Seems that way to me. I think the opportunity presented itself and he grabbed it." He paused at the door of the office building. "It's happened before . . . Hey, why all the interest in Reaves? What's he to you?"

Megan pursed her lips thoughtfully and sidestepped the personal aspects of Ted's pointed question. "An account holder who just might be innocent."

"And might not."

"I'll keep that in mind."

Megan walked into the modern building and stopped to purchase a copy of the *Denver Financial Times* in the lobby. Ted's dark brows quirked. "Don't you subscribe?"

Megan smiled wryly and clutched the paper in a death grip. "This one's for me. Sometimes, after the brokers get through with it, the newspaper is literally torn to pieces."

She and Ted parted at the elevators. Megan stepped into a waiting car and pressed the button for the eighth floor. Ted Benson grabbed a descending elevator that would take him directly to the parking lot and his sleek black Porsche.

The weekend slipped by with no word from Garrett. Not that Megan had expected to hear from him. She hadn't left him Thursday night on the friendliest of terms. And yet, a small, very vital and feminine part of her had hoped that he would call.

She told herself that no news was good news. Hadn't he all but threatened her with a lawsuit? She half expected to hear from Garrett's attorney.

Megan kept herself busy by visiting her father and telling him about the board meeting. He didn't look well, but seemed pleased that she had taken a stand and demanded control of the investment house. Perhaps he was mellowing in what he expected of his daughter. Megan hoped so.

The rest of the weekend she spent studying records for the brokerage firm and worrying about the impending scandal. She was determined in her efforts to forestall any unnecessary rumors.

No account escaped her scrutiny. She worked until two in the morning, reading statements and fortifying herself with hot cups of strong, black coffee. When at last her eyes burned from the strain, she took off her reading glasses and begrudgingly headed for bed.

There, between the cold percale sheets, she desperately tried not to think about Garrett or wonder what she could have shared with him if Patrick's tragic accident and the ensuing scandal hadn't driven them apart.

"Don't torture yourself," she mumbled as she lay restlessly in bed. *Garrett lied to you*, she reminded herself, and married another woman. All those hours alone with him were stolen from Lana Tremaine, the woman Garrett intended to marry all along. Patrick had nothing to do with that.

Sleep was fitful and broken with violent nightmares of a red Jaguar skidding out of control on an icy stretch of road in the middle of the night. The car fishtailed down the mountain highway before ripping through a guardrail and turning end over end down a snow-covered embankment.

Megan's own scream awoke her. She was shaking from the ordeal of the recurring dream. She glanced at the clock. Five in the morning. It was still as dark as the middle of the night. With clammy hands, she grabbed hold of the covers and pulled them more tightly around her neck. Maybe if she concentrated she could fall back to sleep.

After an hour of tossing and turning, she reluctantly pushed the blankets aside and headed for the shower. The hot spray woke her up and relaxed the knots of muscle strain at the base of her neck. She slipped on her robe, made coffee and drank heartily of the black liquid while her eyes scanned the morning edition of the *Denver Herald*.

Nothing on the front page. Even the financial section didn't mention George Samples's scam. Megan breathed a long sigh of relief, settled back in one of the kitchen chairs and sipped her coffee. News of the swindle was sure to break, but the longer it could be put off, the better. It gave her more time to get the facts together and hope that she could determine the extent of George's crime and the identity of his accomplice. Also, it would give her a chance to discover how deeply Garrett was embroiled in the scam.

Though it had been hours since she had eaten, she wasn't hungry. All she could handle for breakfast was a piece of buttered toast. She set the dishes in the dishwasher before returning to the bedroom to get ready for what promised to be a grueling day at the office. Megan expected the story of George's scam to break at any minute, and she wanted to be prepared.

She dressed in a French blue wool suit accented by an ivory silk blouse that tied sedately at her throat. Her coppery hair was twisted into a soft chignon at the base of her neck. The only jewelry she wore were understated Cartier earrings, which added just the right touch of elegance to her otherwise professional attire. When she left the apartment, she was confident that she looked the part of the smart young executive. She had a feeling that today, Monday, the second of November, would be remembered as the day that the solid timbers of McKearn Investments were shaken.

And she was right.

A throng of reporters greeted Megan in the lobby of the office building, much to the aggravation of a security guard who was desperately trying to disperse the uneasy crowd.

"Ms. McKearn," a loud reporter wielding a microphone called to her while ignoring the attempts of the security guard to regain control of the crowd. Megan recognized the faces of some of the wealthy clients of the investment company interspersed with the cameramen, newscasters and newspaper reporters. She had to get hold of the situation.

"I'm sorry about this, Ms. McKearn," the security guard apologized. He was a large man with a winning smile, but today he wasn't smiling and anger snapped in his dark eyes. Megan had known him for years and understood his frustration with the crowd.

"It's all right, Alex," she assured him, and turned

with poise to the anxious reporter advancing upon her.

"Ms. McKearn, please, could you answer a few questions for me?"

Megan smiled confidently. She had to control the growing crowd and create as little of a disturbance as possible. With the clients of McKearn Investments hanging on her every word, it was necessary to handle everyone as politely and efficiently as possible. "Of course I will, but I would prefer to do it upstairs, in my office, where there's a little more privacy—if it's convenient for you."

"It doesn't matter where. As long as I get the story." The reporter with the thick moustache waved to a cameraman shouldering a portable unit.

"The eighth floor," Megan said to the crowd before her throat suddenly constricted. On the outskirts of the noisy mass of bodies stood Garrett. His arrogant eyes and slightly amused smile never left Megan's face. Her heart missed a beat at the sight of him lounging against one of the interior columns supporting the high, brightly tiled ceiling of the lobby of the Jefferson Tower. It was almost as if he were enjoying the spectacle of excitement and confusion.

Was Garrett the cause of this uncomfortable scene? Had he taken it upon himself to inform the press about the investment scam—taking his revenge against her? She felt his eyes searing into her back when she turned abruptly and walked into a waiting elevator car.

The elevator ride was the longest of Megan's life. The tension in the small cubicle as it raced toward the eighth floor was thick and uncomfortable. She felt nervous beads of perspiration between her shoulder blades.

Once she was in her office, however, she fielded the questions hurled at her as if she had done it all her life.

"Ms. McKearn," the reporter with the thick brown moustache shouted. "George Samples is saying that he was framed in some kind of investment scam that originated here at McKearn Investments. Could you comment on his statement?"

Megan was thoughtful for a moment. She was aware of Garrett the moment he sauntered into the room, his sharp hazel eyes missing nothing of the strained confrontation. Megan had to be careful. Anything she might say could be used against her later in court if George Samples, Garrett Reaves, and God only knew who else decided to sue. "It's true that Mr. Samples is no longer with McKearn Investments," she replied evasively. "However, I don't think it would be prudent to discuss the reasons for his departure."

"Wait a minute!" one of the clients objected. "Samples was my broker. What's going on here?"

"Nothing's going on, Mr. Sinclair. Mr. Samples left and Ms. Barnes is taking over his accounts. Unless you would prefer someone else." She hazarded a glance at the television camera and realized that the eyes of the press were still capturing everything she said on film. "I'd like to speak with you later," she suggested with a confident smile, and fortunately Mr. Sinclair said nothing more.

When she turned back toward the bulk of the

crowd, Megan noticed that Garrett had quietly maneuvered himself closer to her. He leaned arrogantly against the bookcase, his angular jaw tense, his strong arms crossed lazily over his chest as he silently observed everything about the unscheduled press conference. Megan looked for a fleeting moment into his incredible, mocking hazel eyes before her attention was forced back to the anxious reporters.

"Ms. McKearn." Another reporter caught Megan's attention. This time it was a short blond woman with suspicious brown eyes. "Mr. Samples indicated that there *is* in fact an investment swindle that originated here—in McKearn Investments. Is there any truth to that rumor?"

A few more reporters began to hurl questions in her direction. Megan held up her palms to the crowd and looked directly into one of the television cameras. "Absolutely none." Megan smiled with feigned equanimity. "Let me take this opportunity to say that no account holder has lost any money on any of the transactions that are currently being investigated—"

"Then there was a scam," the blond surmised with a triumphant gleam in her eye.

"There was an indiscretion or two," Megan allowed. "But our auditors discovered the situation before it got out of hand, and I have personally reviewed all of the accounts to assure our clients of the highest security for their investments."

"Is that meant to let the account holders know that their money is still safe with you?" the blond reporter asked with obvious disbelief. Uncovering a story of this nature could become her springboard into the big time, and she wasn't about to let it slip through her fingers.

"Of course it is." Megan held the young woman's suspicious stare. "I will personally assure it."

"You're reasonably new at running this company, aren't you, Ms. McKearn?" the moustached man interjected.

"I've worked with the investment company for several years—"

"But not as president. And when you took over, you were hired as a temporary replacement for your father, weren't you?"

"My position as president is no longer temporary."

The man didn't listen to her reply. "Well, tell me, do you think that if your father were still running the company, this situation would have occurred?"

Megan glanced nervously at Garrett before answering the question. All trace of amusement had faded from Garrett's angular face. The gleam in his eyes was deadly.

Megan turned her attention back to the reporters. Though seething inside, she managed a tight smile. "I couldn't venture a guess. That situation is purely hypothetical. Now, if you'll excuse me—"she smiled at the hungry members of the press"—I have work to do."

"Well, can you give us any insight on what exactly was going down?" the man persisted.

"Not until the investigation is complete." She turned away from the camera, as if to dismiss the crowd. "Mr. Sinclair?" The thin man nodded. "I'll be right with you."

Begrudgingly, the reporters filed out of Megan's office, and she was left with the task of straightening ruffled feathers and consoling some of McKearn Investments' most prestigious clients. Hazarding a sidelong glance toward the bookcase, she noted that Garrett had exited her office with the last stragglers of the departing press. He must have felt satisfied that he had thrown her day into utter chaos.

Ignoring the renewed sense of betrayal overtaking her, Megan concentrated all of her energy on putting her clients' minds at ease. Marlin Sinclair was easily placated, but Taffeta Peake took more cajoling. The small, eightyish widow sported curly blue-gray hair, brightly colored knit dresses, and had a suspicious mind that was still sharp as a tack. Fortunately, the elderly woman was a loyal person by nature and a close friend to Megan's Aunt Jessica. After nearly an hour of conferring with Megan, Mrs. Peake decided to leave her investments as they were . . . at least for the time being.

The hours hurried by. Megan barely had time to breathe. One after another the company's anxious clients came to call. Just when Megan thought she had finally convinced the last of her worried investors that their money was safe and secure, Garrett strode, unannounced, into her office.

Megan wondered if he'd been waiting for her all day. "You too?" she asked. Just at the sight of him, with his charismatic smile and dark knowing eyes, her hostility began to melt and a slow smile spread across her lips. She read the concern in his warm gaze.

"Wouldn't want you to feel neglected."

Her smile turned into a frown. "No need to worry about that. Not today." The friendly conversation was comforting, and she leaned back in her chair, relaxing slightly from the tension that had been her constant companion ever since waking.

"You haven't been lacking for company?"

"Not for a minute." Her eyes grew serious and she ran her fingers along the edge of the desk. "Tell me something—did you leak what was happening to the press?"

"No." His clear hazel eyes were honest.

Despite her earlier doubts, she knew at once that he was telling the truth. "I didn't think so," she lied.

"Well, at least that's some progress. Now, if you'd just listen to what I've been telling you all along, we could straighten *everything* out." Her pulse jumped at the double meaning.

She hesitated and nervously toyed with a pencil. "I don't think so."

"Why not?"

She shrugged. "Conflict of interest, for starters."

His lips thinned into a dangerous line and he pinched his lower lip pensively between his thumb and forefinger. Dark eyes impaled her. "I don't suppose you've located Samples's accomplice."

She shook her head. A few dark wisps of coppery hair fell out of her coiled chignon. She tucked the wayward strands neatly in place. "I expect that the SEC will find the culprit soon."

"I hope so," Garrett admitted, flopping into a side

chair near the desk and running his gaze appreciatively up the curve of her calf.

"Why's that?"

He smiled the same smile that had touched her in
the past. Decidedly lopsided, showing just the hint
of strong, white teeth, it was nearly boyish in its
charm. That smile could be a devastating weapon
when used to Garrett's advantage. "I think it would
be best if we got this whole stinking scandal behind
us."

"That will take time."

"Not for us, it won't."

Her elegant brows quirked. "What do you mean,
us?"

The smile fell from his face, and for a moment, the
only sound in the room was the quiet ticking of
the antique clock perched on a polished shelf of the
bookcase.

"We've meant too much to each other to have this
kind of a misunderstanding," Garrett said softly,
and Megan's breath caught in her throat.

"Let me get this straight," she whispered. "You
mean that because we were lovers in the past, I
should ignore the fact that your account is under
suspicion?" Her heart was beating a breathless
cadence as what he was suggesting became blind-
ingly clear. "You want me to cover up for
you . . . ?"

Garrett's jaw tensed. His eyes looked boldly into
hers. "There's nothing to cover up, damn it. I'm
only asking for your trust."

She took in a deep breath and lifted her chin.
"You asked for that once before, and I was naïve

enough to believe you," she murmured, knowing for certain that he was using her again, twisting her feelings for him like a knife in her heart.

He pinched the bridge of his nose as if trying to forestall a headache. "Megan, listen," he began, just as a rap on the door announced Ted Benson's arrival. The attorney stepped into the middle of what very obviously was a personal confrontation. His steely eyes took in the scene before him, glanced at the clock and then returned to Megan's angry gaze.

"I'm sorry," Ted apologized stiffly. "Jenny's not at her desk, and I thought we had a meeting scheduled—"

"We do, Ted." Megan turned stone-cold eyes on Garrett. "My business with Mr. Reaves is over."

"I could wait a couple of minutes," Ted suggested without moving toward the door.

"No need." Garrett rose from the chair. "As Ms. McKearn stated, our business is finished—for now." Then, with a possessive swing of his head back toward Megan, he continued. "I'll talk to you later."

Megan didn't bother to respond, but turned all of her attention to the attorney, who was settling in the seat Garrett had just vacated. She didn't watch Garrett's retreat, but she heard the door slam behind him as he exited the tension-filled room.

The sound echoed hollowly in her heart.

Chapter Six

$\mathcal{G}$arrett hadn't misread the look on Ted Benson's face when the attorney walked into Megan's office. It was obvious to Garrett that Ted Benson considered himself more than just the lawyer for McKearn Investments. Benson was interested in Megan as a woman, and just the thought of the stuffy attorney laying a hand on Megan made Garrett's blood boil savagely. Garrett didn't doubt for a minute that the feeling was mutual.

Cursing under his breath, Garrett jammed his hands into the back pockets of his slacks and paced along the short hallway between the investment firm and the elevators. He didn't have to wait long. Within ten minutes, the fiftyish attorney swung out of Megan's office wearing a pained expression on his Ivy League face—an expression he managed to shift to bored nonchalance at the sight of Garrett leaning against the wall near the elevators.

"Still here?" Benson asked, with only the slightest edge to his well-modulated voice.

Garrett nodded stiffly. The less said to the wily attorney, the better.

Ted reached for the elevator call button and hesitated. "I wouldn't press my luck, if I were you."

A slightly crooked and obviously amused smile touched Garrett's lips. His hazel eyes glittered dangerously. "Luck has nothing to do with it, Benson. If I'm pressing anything, it's my advantage."

It was the lawyer's turn to smile. "Have it your way."

"I will."

The elevator doors opened, and with a daring look that silently warned of further, more deadly battles, Ted Benson strode into the waiting car.

Garrett grimaced to himself as the elevator descended. Something about Ted Benson didn't sit well with him. The lawyer's reputation was impeccable, and yet there was something about the emptiness in Benson's stone-cold eyes that bothered Garrett. It was as if the man were out to get him; Garrett had read it in Benson's glare.

He rubbed his chin and chastised himself for his paranoia. *Face it, Reaves,* he cautioned himself, *the man is interested in Megan, and that's what gets to you.* The thought of another man touching Megan did dangerous things to Garrett's mind.

The jingle of keys on a ring caught his attention, and he looked up to see Megan locking the doors of the investment company. She was bent over the door, and the elegant weave of her skirt stretched becomingly over her backside. Garrett eyed the provocative hint of lace that peeked from beneath her skirt, and the gentle curve of her calves. He gritted his teeth together in frustration. What was it about that woman that wouldn't leave him alone? The more he saw of her, the more he wanted. His desire for Megan was becoming an uncontrollable hunger that he suspected would prove to be insatiable.

Megan finished locking the office and turned to face the elevators. She was confronted by Garrett's uncompromising stare.

"I . . . I thought you left," she said, walking toward him, her fingers clenching her briefcase in a death grip. Her raincoat was tossed casually over her arm, and she paused at the elevator to put it on.

"We're not through talking."

Megan sighed. The long day had left her feeling tired and wrung out. "I don't think we really have anything more to discuss." She couldn't hide the worry in her voice. Ted had advised her that the SEC would most likely file a civil suit against all the participants in the scam. Including Garrett.

"Lady, we haven't begun," he assured her as he took her arm and escorted her into the elevator. The twin doors closed and the small car started with a jolt. "I want you to come to the house in Boulder. There are a few things we need to get straight between us."

"We've tried talking before. It didn't work."

"Maybe we just didn't try hard enough."

She shook her head wearily.

"Or maybe the timing was wrong." The elevator shuddered to a stop.

"Timing?"

"You and I should have worked things out three years ago."

Megan strode out of the elevator, conscious of the steely fingers wrapped protectively over her arm. Her pulse was racing dangerously, and she could see by the determined gleam in Garrett's eye and the slant of his jaw that he meant business. "They say that hindsight is twenty-twenty," she observed.

"And they also say that love is better the second time around."

Her steps faltered slightly. "Shows you just how foolish old wives' tales can be . . ."

"Megan. Stop it." He pulled her up short. His dark eyes smoldered. "I don't like playing games. I want you to come home with me."

Outrage flashed in her eyes. "Just like that?"

"Just like that."

"After three years?"

"We need to pick up where we left off."

If only she could believe him. He seemed so honest and so sincere, but the threat of his involvement in the swindle along with his bitter rejection of the past made her cautious. "I'm sorry, Garrett." Slowly she withdrew her arm from the welcome manacle of his grip.

"So am I."

She shook her head at the absurdity of the situation. "I . . . I just can't." When she lifted her eyes they were shadowed in pain. "The house has too many memories that I'd rather not think about."

He smiled sadly and swore a silent oath at himself for his own impetuosity. "Then how about dinner—here, in town? Diablo's?"

"I don't know." What if someone saw them together? The scandal was about to blow wide open. Being caught with one of the suspected participants could ruin her. "I'm not sure that being seen in public would be wise."

"We're just going to dinner, for God's sake. Don't tell me that's suddenly become a crime too."

Megan had to laugh in spite of herself. "Not that I know of. At least, not yet."

"Come on. I'll walk you."

"It must be eight blocks—"

"Give or take a few." He winked broadly, charmingly. The way she remembered him. "The exercise will do you good."

"This is madness, you know," she protested weakly, already caught up in the daring of it.

"This is probably the sanest thing I've done in the last three years." Without much ceremony, he took her briefcase in one hand, her arm in the other, before pushing the glass doors of the building open with his body.

The autumn air was crisp with the promise of snow, and Garrett slipped his arm around her shoulders to warm her. He whispered to her as they walked to the mall and followed it until reaching Larimer Square.

Diablo's was located in a Victorian building flanked by authentic gas lanterns and decorated ornately with gleaming gingerbread. Long ebony shutters flanked paned windows, and a broad front porch welcomed the visitors. Inside, rich wainscoting and muted wallpaper gave a nineteenth-century charm to the renovated building.

Megan and Garrett were led by a liveried waiter to a private room on the second story. The bowed window near the table overlooked one of Denver's oldest—and at one time wildest—streets.

"Why wouldn't you come back to my house?" Garrett asked, once the waiter had delivered the white Burgundy and Garrett had given it his approval.

"I think we'd better keep our relationship strictly professional."

"Why?"

The question startled her. The answer seemed so obvious. She picked up the stemmed wineglass and rotated the cut crystal in her fingers. "What we had was based on a lie, Garrett. The time you and I spent together shouldn't have happened. I can't go back to that house. Too many ghosts from the past live there."

He placed his elbows on the table and rested his chin in his hands to stare at her. His thick brows were pulled together in confusion. "You came last Thursday."

She shook her head and the soft light from the lantern shimmered in the red streaks of her hair. "I was coerced."

"By me?"

She nodded. "And it didn't accomplish anything."

He seemed about to protest just as the waiter came into the room and silently placed a steaming platter laden with broiled trout and wild rice onto the table. Only after the dark-haired waiter disappeared did the tense conversation resume.

"We need some time together," he said.

"Because you're in trouble."

"Because I want to be with you." The rueful slant of his mouth suggested that he was telling the truth.

"Why, Garrett? Why now? After three years?"

"Because I'm tired of paying for my mistakes."

Like the mistake you made when you joined forces with George Samples, Megan thought, and her suspicion must have shown on her face.

"This has nothing to do with the situation at the investment company," he said quietly.

Her gray eyes glinted like newly forged steel. Just how gullible did he think she was? "Don't lie to me, Garrett," she whispered. "I may have believed everything you told me once, but I'm not that stupid anymore. If George's scam hadn't come to light, we wouldn't be here tonight."

"Maybe not tonight. But that doesn't alter the fact that I want to be with you."

"It only embellishes it."

"Oh, Megan, can't you make the effort to trust me—just for a little while?"

I did once, she reminded herself, and it ended in disaster. "It's not that easy, not now."

"Too many ghosts, is that it?"

She nodded mutely and pretended interest in her meal. Looking at Garrett was only making it harder to say no. The honesty in his hazel eyes was nearly her undoing. The hard, familiar angle of his jaw and the easy manner in which he stared into her eyes was a sensual invitation—a difficult one for Megan to resist.

He leaned back in his chair, tossed his napkin aside and studied her. "I think you're making excuses, Megan. The truth of the matter is that you're *afraid* of being alone with me."

"I just don't think it would be wise."

"That didn't stop you before."

"I guess I'm a little more careful now."

"Jaded, you mean."

She lifted her shoulders and wrapped her trembling fingers around the stem of her wineglass. He was getting to her. The intimate meal, the heady wine and the persistence in his bold eyes were beginning to touch a part of her she would have preferred to keep hidden. Reason and composure were escaping in the seductive atmosphere of the room.

When the meal was finished and the check was paid, both she and Garrett lingered at the table, as if they were afraid to go any further with the night. Where could it lead? What would happen if she gave in to the persistent questions in his eyes?

Reluctantly Megan followed Garrett down the sweeping staircase of the old manor. Her fingers slid easily along the polished oak rail as she descended. She was on the last step, when her eyes met those of a moustached man standing near the bar. Recognition flashed across the young man's face.

"Ms. McKearn?" he asked, stepping away from an attractive brunette and a frothy mug of beer.

Megan paused, trying to place the face. Garrett

stopped and watched the young man with suspicious eyes. Megan could feel her pulse beginning to quicken.

"I'm Harold Dansen from KRCY news." He seemed disappointed that she didn't remember him. "I interviewed you this morning."

Megan's heart hit the floor, but the brash young man ignored her obvious discomfiture. "I'd like a private interview with you." When she didn't immediately respond, he pressed his point home. "You know what I mean: a more personal story about you, your family, how you got to be president of the company, what McKearn Investments' position on this investment scam *really* is. That sort of thing."

"I'll let you know," Megan replied vaguely, just as Garrett stepped closer to her side and cut off any more of the anxious reporter's questions.

Flinty eyes moved from Megan to Garrett and back again, and the reporter smiled in obvious satisfaction. "Hey, you're Garrett Reaves."

The McKearn Investments story had just become a lot more interesting to Harold Dansen. Garrett Reaves was a man who valued his privacy. A very wealthy man who scorned public attention. And Reaves was here, with the president of McKearn Investments, a company whose credibility was dropping faster than a stone in water. To top matters off, Megan McKearn looked very disturbed that she had been recognized with Reaves. The story made for interesting copy—very interesting copy indeed. Harold Dansen noticed the angry gleam in Reaves's eyes and warned himself to be careful.

Discreetly, Garrett took Megan's arm and propelled her toward the door. An interview with the likes of Dansen now would be a disaster.

"Wait a minute," Dansen demanded.

Megan couldn't afford to anger the press, and yet she knew that she had to sidestep Dansen and his pointed questions. She looked over her shoulder and graced him with her most winning smile. "I'll call you," she promised. "Harold Dansen, KRCY, right?"

Harold nodded, struck for a moment by her intriguing beauty. Megan McKearn was a woman who could turn heads with only the flash of her delicate smile. He watched her walk out of Diablo's and noticed Garrett's proprietary hand on her arm.

Harold Dansen smelled the hottest story to hit Denver in over a year.

"You're a liar," Garrett accused as he drove through the dark streets of Denver. He had walked Megan back to the Jefferson Tower and then had insisted that he drive Megan home. She had reluctantly agreed, and they were now seated in his silver BMW. The first snowflakes of winter were falling from the black sky, and the interior of the car was cold.

"What do you mean?"

"You have no intention of calling that Dansen character. At least I hope you have more brains than that."

"I didn't lie," Megan laughed. "I will call him. I'm just not sure when."

"After all the publicity has died down, unless I miss my guess. When that happens, KRCY won't be interested in McKearn Investments." Garrett smiled and let out a low laugh. "And you used to tell me *I* equivocated."

"It's not quite the same thing as lying."

"Just a fancier word."

Garrett drove directly to the town house where she had lived for the past five years, one of several tall, nineteenth-century-looking row houses joined by common walls. After finding a parking place on the sloped street, Garrett helped Megan out of the car.

The snow had begun in earnest, and powdery flakes were giving an eerie illumination to the dark night as they fell past the glowing streetlamps. Megan's breath caught in her throat before condensing in the cold night air.

"Would you like to come in for a minute?" she asked, and felt an embarrassed tinge color her cheeks. "I could get you a drink . . . or a cup of coffee . . ."

Garrett's smile was wistful. He watched her struggle with the words. "I've been waiting for an invitation like that all night."

Ignoring the huskiness of his voice and the deeper meaning in his words, Megan unlocked the door, stepped into the hallway and flipped on the lights. She tossed her coat onto a chair near the closet and walked into the kitchen.

Garrett followed her at a slower pace, his eyes looking into the rooms, which were only vaguely familiar. He had only been to her home once before, and that was nearly three years ago. He remembered the polish of the gleaming hardwood floors, the

Italian marble on the fireplace, the bright patina of the antique brass bed . . .

By the time he passed by the staircase and entered the kitchen, Megan had poured two cups of coffee laced with brandy. Garrett noticed that the snowflakes that had clung to her hair were melting. Her cheeks were flushed from the cold, and silvery anticipation sparked in her eyes.

Garrett took off his coat and accepted the warm mug she offered before following her into the living room. The room was small, decorated with an eclectic blend of solid wooden antiques and several overstuffed pieces in rich tones of dusty rose and ivory.

Megan took a seat on the padded couch and tucked her feet under her. She took an experimental sip of the brandied coffee and observed Garrett as he set his drink on a small table, took off his jacket, loosened his tie and set to the task of building a fire from the kindling and paper sitting in a basket on the hearth.

"You don't have to—" Megan began to protest, but stilled her tongue. For a strange reason, she was pleased by the thought of Garrett building a fire in her home. It made him seem as if he belonged here, and she found the idea comforting, if slightly dangerous.

It took a few minutes, but soon the room was filled with the scent of burning pitch and the crackle of flames as they consumed the dry wood. Garrett dusted his hands and sat on the edge of the hearth, letting the warmth of his efforts heat his back. "It should be a law that you have to build a fire during the first snowfall," he decided as he reached for his drink. He took a long, satisfying swallow of the blend of brandy and coffee and watched the snowflakes begin to mound on the window ledge.

"Garrett?" The tone of her voice brought his eyes crashing back to meet the uneasiness in hers. "Why don't we quit stalling and get right down to the reason you're here?"

His friendly smile slowly disappeared. "I wanted to see you again."

She took a sip from her mug and shook her head before leaning wearily against the plump cushions of the rose-colored couch. "Why?"

A muscle worked in the corner of his jaw. "Because it's obvious that you don't trust me, and I think I can understand why," he stated with a sigh. "But you'd better face facts, lady. You're in this as deeply as I am."

"So we'd better form some sort of alliance, is that it?"

His dark eyes flashed with angry gold sparks and the brackets surrounding his mouth deepened cynically. "I think I owe you an explanation."

"About how you got involved with Samples?"

He pondered the black liquid swirling in the bottom of his cup. "About how I got involved with Lana Tremaine."

Megan's throat went dry. The old pain of betrayal cut into her heart. "Maybe we shouldn't bring up the past," she suggested. What would it accomplish? Old wounds would only be reopened. "It's over and done with."

"I don't think so." He finished his drink in one

swallow, straightened and strode over to the couch. "There's a lot you don't understand," he stated, touching the curve of her jaw with a sensitive finger.

She held up her palm to forestall the attack on her senses. The conversation was becoming too personal and dangerous. All at once she wanted to crawl back into the safe cocoon of her life and forget about the past. Garrett read the regret in her wide gray eyes.

"I handled everything wrong."

"And now you want to atone for your mistakes?" Megan couldn't hide the bitter sound of disbelief that had entered her voice.

"Let me say what I have to, Megan." He shook his head at the wonder of her. "You never were very good at listening."

"Maybe that was because you weren't very good at confiding in me."

"It wasn't intentional—"

"Not intentional?" she echoed with tears beginning to well in her eyes. "How could you forget the fact that you were engaged to another woman while conducting an . . . an affair with me?"

"Lana and I had called it off—"

"You never even mentioned her," Megan protested, tears of anguish starting to burn in her throat.

"It wasn't something I wanted to dwell on. I assumed you knew about her."

"No one saw fit to tell me." Gray, condemning eyes studied the rugged planes of his handsome face. "Until—"

"Until it was too late," he finished for her, following the path of her thoughts. "Is that what you thought it was between us . . . a mistake?"

"Yes."

"Oh, lady," he murmured, edging closer to her on the couch. His hand reached upward and slowly removed the pins from her hair. At the intimacy of the gesture her lower lip trembled and she closed her eyes. "Knowing you was never a mistake."

"Don't—"

"Shhh. It's time you listened to me." She felt the whisper-soft touch of his fingers against the curve of her jaw. Tears burned her eyelids in wistful remembrance. *How could anything once so beautiful turn so painful in the course of a few short hours?*

His fingers toyed with the ruffle of her blouse, lingering over the pulsing hollow of her throat. And his eyes, vibrant green streaked with brilliant gold, touched the most intimate part of her.

Despite the pain, despite the lonely years, despite Garrett's betrayal, Megan wasn't immune to the seductiveness of his touch. The feel of his fingers toying with the collar of her blouse made her pulse quicken and her heart begin to pound. Thoughts of a younger, more innocent time, before the tragic night of Patrick's death, began to flirt with her mind.

His fingers caught in the fiery strands of her hair and felt for the nape of her neck. "You're a very beautiful woman, Megan," he whispered as his eyes caressed the refined contours of her face. "Even more beautiful than I remembered."

He was touching her, disturbing rational thought, and a small but very vital part of her was exhilarated by the knowledge that he still wanted her. Her voice, a throaty whisper, was filled with the ache of raw emotions. "I don't think it would be wise to get involved again."

"Too late," he murmured, moving nearer to her. His breath whispered across her hair. "I'm already involved."

She intended to push him away, but the fingers pressed urgently against his chest were little barrier against his weight as he slowly let his body cover hers.

His lips brushed gingerly against the column of her throat before moving upward against the silken texture of her skin. He groaned as the familiar scent of her perfume invaded his nostrils and his fingers twined in the soft waves of her auburn hair. When his lips found hers, the passion of his kiss bridged the black abyss of three forgotten years.

Megan's breathing was irregular, and the weight of Garrett's body, crushing against her rising and falling breasts, was the sweetest aphrodisiac she had ever known. The familiarity of his scent, the seduction in his hazel eyes, the sensual quirk of his dark brows made her ache for him as wantonly as she had in the past.

She welcomed the urgent pressure of his tongue against her teeth, and without hesitation she parted her mouth to accept his warm invasion. Savoring the taste of him, Megan sighed expectantly when his fingers reached for the buttons on her blouse.

Slowly, applying the most excruciatingly sweet torture possible, he slid the pearl buttons from their bonds to part the silken fabric and touch the delicate flesh near her collarbone. The creamy blouse slid off her shoulders and onto the floor while his fingers surrounded the swell of one lace-covered breast. The cool night air coupled with the warmth of his touch made her breasts ache and her nipples tighten under the tender persuasion of his gentle fingers.

"Garrett, please," Megan whispered as the sweet agony enveloped her. The silk and lace of her camisole slid seductively over her breasts, and the thin strap holding the frail garment fell off her shoulder, exposing more of the velvet softness of her skin to him. He kissed the rounded swell of her breast before letting his lips hover over one expectant nipple.

She sighed and wound her fingers in the coarse strands of his heavy hair as she felt the wet impression of his tongue against her skin. Cradling the back of his head and holding him tightly against her breast, she moaned as he suckled her gently through the moistened fabric. Her breathing was raspy, and she couldn't find the strength to stop him when he unbuttoned the waistband of her skirt and slid it over her hips to let it fall, unnoticed, to the floor.

Sweat beaded on Garrett's brow as he surveyed the woman lying seductively beneath him on the couch. Megan's eyes were glazed with a passion only he could spark, and the rapid whisper of her breath through her parted lips invited him to take all of her.

The lacy cream camisole clung erotically to her body, conforming to the rounded contours of her figure. Auburn hair streaked with jets of flaming red surrounded a perfect oval face that was flushed with the heat of intimate passion. Shadowy lashes lowered seductively over silvery eyes. Dark nipples, hard with desire, peaked through the scanty lace, beckoning with rosy invitation.

He groaned as his head lowered to touch them with tip of his tongue. Megan closed her eyes and abandoned herself to him. Gone with the day were all of the doubts that had plagued her, replaced by the night and the need for his gentle touch. Her body arched intimately against his, aching for the familiar feel of his skin pressed urgently against hers.

Her fingers found the buttons of his shirt, and they trembled as she slowly parted the soft cotton fabric. The shirt fell open, exposing the muscles, rock-hard and lean, that moved fluidly over one another as he raised his body from hers, unbuttoned his cuffs and tossed the unwanted shirt over the back of the couch.

Tentatively her fingers touched his chest. He pulled her hand away and pressed his tongue into her palm. Dark eyes held hers fast, and her blood ran in heated waves throughout her body when his tongue flickered between her fingers.

"I want you," he murmured, his voice thick with the promise of unleashed passion. Those same words echoed from the past, and touched a dangerous part of her mind.

"I . . . I don't know if that's enough," she gasped, trying to reach for rational thought.

"Let me love you." He leaned over her again, and she felt the pressure of his hard torso crushing her breasts. His breath caressed her face, and his eyes, bright with unleashed desire, drove steadily into hers. She felt as if he were reading her darkest secrets. "Let it happen, Megan."

The palm of his hand slid beneath the satiny fabric of her camisole and cupped her breast. Megan gasped as his fingers toyed with her nipple, creating a whirlpool of hot desire deep within the most feminine part of her soul.

His lips touched hers, and his tongue outlined her parted mouth before his head lowered and he placed the warmth of his mouth over the exposed breast. Megan took in a shuddering breath and didn't object when she felt him shift off the couch to encircle her body with his arms.

In one sure movement he stood and carried her out of the living room and up the graceful staircase to the second floor. First one shoe and then the other dangled from her toes to drop unheeded on the staircase.

Garrett stared steadily into her eyes, silently demanding answers to the unasked questions of the past.

It would be so easy to fall in love with this man again, she thought. So easy and so dangerous. Why hadn't she learned her lesson? How could she contemplate letting him into her life again when so many painful years stood between them?

He carried her into the shadowy bedroom and didn't bother with the lights. She felt the hardness of his mouth as he kissed her again, and desire ripped through her body in white-hot spasms. His tongue probed into her mouth forcefully, touching each intimate part of her with renewed determination and mastery.

She felt the cool polish of the satin comforter against her back when he placed her firmly on the bed. As his dark eyes held hers, he deftly removed the rest of her clothes and tossed them carelessly onto the floor.

His eyes never left her face as he unclasped his belt buckle and slowly removed his pants. Within seconds, he had stripped himself of his clothes and walked boldly back to the bed.

As he lowered himself onto the antique brass bed, Megan felt the sag of the mattress and the welcome warmth of his body covering hers. Her fingers splayed around his back and gently traced the supple curve of each muscle.

The lips he pressed against hers were hard and demanding. No longer was he asking for her compliance; he was taking what he felt was rightfully his. And she didn't deny him.

Megan felt the exquisite wonder of his hands as they molded against her body, and she realized that her need of him had become white-hot with desire. He touched her legs, letting his fingers slide erotically up her calf and thigh until she moaned from the torment of the hot void aching within her.

His weight, when he pressed against her, was a pleasant burden. His hands offered both torment and solace to her anxious body, and his tongue— God, his tongue!—danced deliciously over her skin until she writhed with the passion flooding her mind and washing over the most intimate parts of her.

"Garrett, please," she moaned against his shoulder. She tasted the salt of his sweat when her mouth touched his skin, and she sighed in grateful relief when at last, she felt his knee part her legs and the firm gift of his manhood joined with her.

The coupling was strong and heated. Words of love, lost in the wonder of the night, sprang unbidden from her lips. And when the final moment of climactic surrender bound them, Megan knew that she was a woman powerless against her love for this man.

Chapter Seven

$\mathscr{P}$ale morning light filtered through the sheer curtains and partially illuminated the quaint room with the silvery iridescence of dawn. Memories, filled visual images of passion and satiation, sifted through Garrett's mind. He squeezed his eyes tightly shut and smiled as thoughts of last night invaded his senses. He felt younger than he had in years. Megan's body was pressed against his back. Garrett stretched before rolling onto his side to watch her cuddle against him without waking.

A pale green sheet was seductively draped across her breasts, and the satin comforter had slipped from the bed to the floor. One of her arms rested comfortably across Garrett's chest. Garrett grinned to himself and brushed aside a lock of auburn hair that had fallen over her cheek. Her dark lashes fluttered open and her eyes, heavy with sleep, opened slowly.

"Garrett?" she whispered, her elegant brows drawing together in confusion before she remembered the events of the evening. She smiled up at him lazily, thinking that she was alone in bed with the only man she had ever loved.

"You're beautiful," he said, his eyes holding hers. "I could get used to this."

Megan was running her fingers through her tousled hair when reality struck her like a bolt of lightning. "My God, what time is it?" Bracing herself on one elbow, she peered over his body to the antique sewing machine that served as a nightstand.

Garrett grinned broadly as she held her hair out of her face and squinted at the alarm clock. A dark frown creased her forehead when she read the digital display.

"I've got to get up . . ."

"You're not going anywhere," he protested, his hands wrapping possessively over her wrists.

"It's nearly eight!"

"And I can't think of a better place to start the morning than here."

Megan's eyes were earnest. "Neither can I," she admitted, trying to withdraw her hands from his grasp. "But I should be at the office in ten minutes."

"You'll never make it."

"Not unless you let go of me." She saw the teasing light in his eyes and tried to diffuse it. "Look, Garrett, the New York Stock Exchange is already up and running. And, with all the bad press the investment house is getting, I can't afford to be late—"

"You already are."

"Not for long." She attempted to pull free of his embrace, but he pulled on her arms and her torso followed. Soon she was lying atop him and all she had succeeded in accomplishing was to be drawn closer to him. Her dark hair tumbled in disheveled curls around her face, and she looked at him with mock consternation. "Don't *you* have somewhere you're supposed to be?" she asked, changing tactics and appealing to his sense of responsibility.

"Um-hum." His lips touched hers provocatively. "Right here."

"What about your company?"

"They can get along without me for a few hours." His hands rubbed suggestively up her spine, and she knew she was losing the battle.

"You're impossible," she said with a sigh.

"And you love it."

"Garrett, be serious."

"I am."

"I *have* to get to work."

"What you *have* to do, lady, is talk to me."

"There's no time." She lifted her finger and touched his beard-roughened cheek.

"Make time," he suggested, kissing the finger that had caressed his cheek.

"Can't we talk later?" She slid a glance of seductive speculation in his direction. "Or was this just a one-night stand?"

He stiffened beneath her. "You know better than that."

"Then it can wait."

Garrett hesitated. "I want to explain about Lana —and for once, I want you to listen."

A painful shadow crossed her eyes and her frail smile turned wistful. She closed her eyes for a moment and fought against the tears that always threatened whenever she thought about Garrett's betrayal. "Maybe we should avoid that topic."

Something in his eyes turned cold. "I just want you to understand that I never loved Lana. The marriage was a mistake from the beginning."

"Then why, Garrett?" Megan asked suddenly, the question she had asked herself for nearly three years springing from her lips.

He rolled his eyes heavenward. "I wish I knew," he admitted. "At the time, I thought it was the right move. You never wanted to see me again." A quick shake of his head stilled the protests forming on her lips. "And I really couldn't blame you." He closed his eyes as if against a sudden stab of pain. "I should have told you that I had been engaged to her, but . . ." He let out a disgusted breath. "The timing never seemed right. I guess I took the coward's way out. You know the old adage, what she doesn't know won't hurt her. The more involved I was with you, the less my relationship with Lana mattered."

"But you still married her," Megan whispered, her eyes bright with unshed tears.

His jaw hardened and defeat saddened his gaze. "She was waiting for me. When you shoved me out of your life, she was there." He cradled the back of his dark head and stared at the ceiling. "It doesn't make it right," he admitted, his voice rough, "but that's the way it happened."

"I thought we meant so much to each other," Megan whispered.

"So did I." His voice was cold. "But after Patrick's accident, you wouldn't return my calls. You wouldn't have anything to do with me." His voice lowered and he was forced to clear his throat. "It seemed obvious to me that you wanted me out of your life—for good," he added, turning his head to look at her.

"It was a difficult time for me," she hedged, averting her eyes from his penetrating gaze. There were so many things she wanted to tell him—so many things he couldn't begin to understand.

Garrett shifted on the bed, sensing that Megan was shutting him out. "Megan, talk to me."

"I will," she promised huskily, silently hoping for a little time to put her scattered thoughts in order. Last night she had been swept away in the heated tides of passion. This morning she was forced back to reality. The bitter pain of the past and the suspicions of today. Not once had Garrett mentioned the investment swindle, but Megan couldn't forget that he might very well be involved in the scam. "But I don't want to rush it," she insisted. "Right now I've got to get ready for work." She swallowed back the tears and managed a tight smile before laying a comforting hand on his shoulder. "I didn't mean to push you away back then, Garrett. It's just that there were so many things I didn't understand. . . . Patrick's death was very confusing." Slipping off the bed, she reached for her robe and wrapped it tightly around her body despite the protesting sound from Garrett.

Before he could say anything else, she hurried into the bathroom, where she showered, applied a little makeup and pinned her hair in place. Her thoughts lingered on the man she loved. The night had been an intriguing blend of romance, mystery and seduction.

As she stared sightlessly into the steamy mirror, she wondered if it were possible that he loved her—just a little. He obviously cared; she could read that in the stormy depths of his dark, brooding gaze. At the thought of his erotic eyes, her pulse began to quiver and she had to force herself not to run back into the bedroom and into his waiting arms. There were too many barriers standing between them. Not only the past separated them, but also Garrett's involvement in the investment scam. Though he still protested his innocence, he *had* threatened to sue McKearn Investments. Her teeth sunk into her lower lip. She doubted that he would use her to his advantage, but she had only to consider the past to realize what he could do if he felt cornered.

She set down the hairbrush. Perhaps he was right. Maybe they should talk things over and clear the air. If she lost him now it would hurt, but she could pull herself together again. If her involvement with him deepened, the pain would only be worse.

With new resolve, she stepped into the creamy robe and decided to face the truth. Garrett was right. Before she could begin to trust him completely, they would have to discuss his brief marriage to Lana Tremaine as well as the potential lawsuit. The story he had just told her didn't quite jibe with Lana's version.

Her heart was hammering when she opened the door to the bedroom. "I think it would be best if we talked," Megan announced—to the empty room. Her hand was still poised on the bathroom door and her eyes scanned the small bedroom. Garrett's clothes were missing. Hers had been neatly folded and placed on the freshly made bed. With a lump in her throat, she realized that Garrett might have left her . . . again.

She turned when she heard a noise behind her, and then smiled when she realized that Garrett was still in the house. He was mounting the stairs two at a time. When he dashed into the room, he was wearing only his slacks and unbuttoned shirt. The exposed muscles of his chest were taut. Tucked under his arm he carried the morning edition of the *Denver Herald*.

"I think you'd better get dressed," he said tersely as he handed her the folded newspaper."

"Why . . . what's happened?" she asked, noting the wariness in his dark gaze, the strain of his muscles as he began buttoning his shirt.

"Page one," was the clipped reply.

Megan opened the newspaper with trembling fingers and her throat became suddenly arid. In bold, angry letters, the headlines read:

MCKEARN INVESTMENTS
TIED TO SWINDLE

Broker Claims He Was Framed

George Samples, an investment counselor for McKearn Investments, stated yesterday that he was framed in an investment scam originating at the Denver-based brokerage. Samples declared that he is an innocent party to the swindle, which includes several of his accounts.

When asked about Samples's allegations, the president of McKearn Investments, Megan Mc-Kearn, declined comment. Ms. McKearn inherited the position of president of the eighty-year-old investment company from her father, Jedediah McKearn, who successfully ran the business for nearly forty years. Mr. McKearn, who is semiretired, was unavailable for comment concerning the alleged framing and subsequent dismissal of Samples. According to Samples, the Securities and Exchange Commission is investigating the situation.

"Oh, no," Megan whispered, her eyes scanning the column. Along with the biased text were two pictures. One was of a stern-faced George Samples and another fellow, captioned as George's attorney. The second picture was a snapshot of Jed, taken several years ago when he was still running the company.

Without reading any further, Megan tossed the offensive paper onto the bed and called her parents.

The line was busy. She tried again. The monotonous signal beeped in her ear. "Dear God, why won't they leave him alone?" she whispered as she replaced the receiver and shuddered as if from a sudden chill.

Garrett came over to the edge of the bed and placed a strong arm over her shoulders. "You knew it would come to this," he said, trying to calm her.

"Damn!" Megan's small fist crashed forcefully on the sewing machine before she picked up the receiver again and angrily punched out the number for McKearn Investments.

After several rings, a ragged-sounding Jenny answered the phone.

Megan identified herself, and she could hear the relief in the receptionist's voice. "The press has been calling all morning, but I wouldn't give them your number," Jenny stated with a sigh.

Silently Megan cursed her private listing. No wonder the reporters were hounding her father. "That's good, Jenny," Megan said, despite inner fears. "Tell the reporters that I'll be in later in the day and I'll make a statement at that time. Then please call Ted Benson and tell him I'll stop by his office if he's free—I'll check back with you to get the time. Right now, I'm going over to visit my father. If you need me, you can reach me there."

"What about the clients?" Jenny asked hesitantly.

"Each broker should deal with his own. I will personally speak with any of George's clients when I get to the office. I'll call you in a couple of hours."

With her final statement, Megan hung up the phone and tried to call her parents one last time. The line was still busy. "Great," she muttered under her breath, only partially aware that Garrett was watching her.

"Let me drive you," Garrett suggested as he saw the concern etched in Megan's face.

She shook her head. "I don't think that would be wise— Oh, damn!"

"What?"

"I left my car at the office."

Garrett stood and tucked the tails of his shirt into his slacks. "Look, Megan, I'll take you to Jed's house. But I think we'd better hurry. No doubt the reporters are knocking on his door this morning."

Without further argument, Megan reached for a heather-colored wool skirt and matching sweater. She tugged on gray boots and slung a tweed jacket over her shoulders before racing down the stairs and out into the bright, snow-covered morning.

It took nearly twenty minutes for Garrett to maneuver the BMW across town. Most of the streets were passable, but the overnight accumulation of the first snow of winter made driving more difficult than it had been since early spring. Though the day was clear and a brilliant sun radiated from a blue sky, Megan shivered with dread. The newspaper was tucked under her arm, the condemning article hidden by the folds of newsprint.

Megan's fingers tapped anxiously on the armrest of the car, and her face was strained as she stared out the window. How would her father react to the article? Would a bevy of reporters be camped on Jed's doorstep? If it weren't for his failing health . . .

Megan swallowed back the rising dread in her throat.

The wheels of Garrett's car spun for a minute as he turned into the long drive of the McKearn estate. Megan noticed the fresh tracks in the snow. At least one reporter was already there. Through the pine trees, brilliant flashes of red and white light caught her attention. Megan's heart felt as if it had stopped beating.

"Oh, my God," she whispered when she first set eyes on the ambulance parked near the garage. It was facing the street, its lights reflecting ominously in the pristine stillness of the snowfall. "Dad . . ." A few other cars were parked near the house, and people, mostly from the press, had collected near the doorway. Megan didn't notice them.

Garrett drove toward the ambulance, and Megan reached for the handle of the door before the car had completely stopped. A strong hand over her arm arrested her. "Megan, brace yourself," Garrett advised. She stared for a moment into his concerned eyes and then opened the car door and hurried toward the house. She heard Garrett's footsteps behind her.

Questions were tossed in her direction.

"Ms. McKearn, what's going on?"

"Is there something wrong with your father? Rumor has it that he collapsed this morning."

"Did he know about the investment swindle?"

"Ms. McKearn?"

Muffled voices. Obscured whispers. Pieces of a conversation drifted to her ears over the sound of her boots crunching in the snow.

"Hey—who's she with?" a husky voice inquired. "Doesn't that guy look like—"

"Garrett Reaves. Wasn't she involved with him a a few years back?" was the higher-pitched response.

"Don't know. That's about the time her brother was killed."

"Oh, yeah, now I remember—and a girl too, right?"

"And Reaves was involved then, too? Hey—this is looking better all the time." Then louder, "Ms. McKearn. If I could have just a few minutes . . . ?"

But she was already near the back door. She hadn't heard most of the questions, and those that had met her ears she ignored. Her father's life was on the line. Nothing else mattered. The same sick feeling that had overtaken her the night Patrick was killed had returned.

Megan's gray eyes were deadly when she turned them on the curious reporters. "Just leave me and my family alone," Megan cast over her shoulder as she jerked open the door. For a moment she thought she caught a glimpse of Harold Dansen, but she quickly forgot the reporter for KRCY as her worry and dread mounted.

Inside, the house was mayhem. Two attendants were wheeling a stretcher toward the door. On it was Jed, his face ashen, the lines of age wrinkling his once robust skin.

"What's happening here?" Megan demanded of one attendant. "I'm Jed's daughter."

Anna McKearn, her red hair unkempt around her swollen face, intervened. "They think he's had another attack," Megan's mother choked out. "Thank God you're here."

"We're taking him to Mercy," the attendant stated as Jed was wheeled out of the house. "You can ride with us."

Anna nodded.

"Wait, Mom. I'll come with you."

"Sorry, lady. No room," the larger attendant said. He turned to his partner. "Let's move."

Megan hugged her mother quickly before Anna followed the attendants out. She stood in the doorway and watched the ambulance roar out of the driveway, siren screaming and lights flashing.

Most of the reporters had taken Megan's angry advice. The more persistent journalists had lingered, only to be told by Garrett that there would be no comment on anything until Jed's condition had stabilized.

Garrett was leaning against his car when Megan emerged from the house some ten minutes later with a few of Jed's belongings packed into an overnight case. "Dad might need these," she explained feebly, fearing that Jed might never have the opportunity to use the shaving kit and pajamas.

She slid into the car and fought against the tears of despair filling her eyes. Garrett placed his hand over hers, then turned the car around and headed for Mercy Hospital.

"Heart attack?" Garrett asked, softly.

Megan nodded mutely and stared out the window at the snow-covered city. She felt suddenly empty and completely helpless.

The next few minutes seemed like hours until the

stark concrete hospital building came into view. Garrett parked near the emergency entrance and helped Megan out of the car. The snow had been shoveled from the parking lot, and Megan walked briskly toward the building. Garrett walked with her, his face set in a grim mask of determination.

Anna McKearn met her daughter in the waiting area. Her face was pale, and for the first time in her life she looked her fifty-six years.

"How bad is it?" Megan wanted to know.

Anna's blue eyes held her daughter's for a second and then slid anxiously away from Megan's probing stare. But in that silent, chilling moment when their eyes collided, Megan knew that her father wasn't expected to live. Tears formed in her eyes, but she forced them back, hoping to find courage against the grim situation.

"What happened?" she finally asked.

Anna tried to speak, couldn't, and just shook her head. Megan gripped her mother's hand firmly, and silently wondered if Jed's heart attack had been triggered by the series of events exploding around the investment company. Jed was under doctor's orders to avoid stress, and the events of the last few days must have put pressure on his frail condition.

The wait was tedious. After about an hour, a young doctor with thick glasses took a chair near Megan's mother. From the defeated expression on the doctor's boyish face, Megan realized that her father was gone.

A strangled cry erupted from Anna's throat before she managed to pull herself together and listen to Dr. Walker. He explained that the resuscitation attempts on Jed had failed. He had never regained consciousness, and his heart had given out completely shortly after he arrived at the hospital.

Megan was stricken and felt a burning nausea rise in her stomach. Though she had known her father's condition was weak, she had never really considered how empty her life would be without him. A cold, black void of loneliness loomed before her.

After holding her mother for a few minutes, Megan found her voice. "I think we should go home. . . . I'll stay with you."

"I'll . . . I'll be fine," Anna sniffed, squaring her shoulders, but beneath the show of bravado in Anna's blue eyes, Megan recognized disbelief and despair.

"Come on. We have a lot to do." Somehow, despite her own loss, Megan was able to lend her mother a strong arm on which to lean.

Garrett had witnessed the painful scene from a distance. When Anna was on her feet, he offered her a cup of coffee.

"I don't think so," she said with a weary frown.

"Then let me drive you and Megan home."

"I don't want to inconvenience you," Anna replied. "Megan can call a cab."

"Please," Garrett insisted, and Anna McKearn accepted his offer quietly.

Once back at the house, it took Megan several hours to convince her mother to rest. In the meantime, Megan had called the office twice, arranging to have her car driven to her mother's home and promising that she would be in no later than tomorrow morning.

Jenny assured her that, under the circumstances, the staff could work one day without Megan's presence.

Garrett stayed just long enough to convince himself that both Megan and her mother were able to care for themselves.

"You'll call me if you need me?" he said softly as he was leaving.

"I'll be fine," Megan assured him. She was dog tired, but tried to hide that fact from Garrett. He, too, looked as if he could sleep for two solid days.

"And your mother?"

"She's stronger than you might think. I've already called Aunt Jessica. She'll be here in the morning to help with the funeral arrangements and take care of Mom. I'll stay here for a couple of days—until I know that Mom's okay." Megan leaned against the bookcase near the entry, but she had to look away from a framed photograph of her father and brother, which was sitting at eye level on a nearby shelf. The snapshot had been taken when Patrick was only fifteen.

Garrett's hand reached out and touched her chin, forcing her to look directly into his eyes. "And how about you—are you okay?"

She couldn't lie. Instead, she shook her head regretfully, and the tears she had silently kept at bay filled her eyes. "I will be—in a few days."

"You're sure?"

She forced the tears back and smiled sadly. "Of course I will. It just takes a little time."

His eyes lingered on her worried face. "Would you like me to stay?"

She couldn't answer at once. Too many feelings were storming within her, and the loss of her father ached deeply in her heart. First Patrick. Now her father. All of the men who mattered in her life were gone . . . except for Garrett. And she couldn't stay with him. Not until some of the angry pain had subsided. "Not tonight, Garrett," she whispered, praying that he would understand.

He smiled sadly before bending over to place a tender kiss on her lips. "I'll call," he promised before walking out of the house.

When the door closed behind him, Megan slumped against the cold wood and released the quiet tears of grief that had been burning against her eyelids for the better part of the day.

Chapter Eight

The week sped crazily by. Between the turmoil at the office, the continued onslaught of reporters interested in unraveling all of the sordid details of the swindle, the SEC investigation, and care for her grieving mother, Megan didn't have a moment's peace. From the minute she woke up each morning until she dropped wearily into bed late at night, Megan had no time to herself. It was as if her entire world were beginning to crumble and fall, piece by piece.

She didn't see Garrett again until the funeral. The crowd of mourners attending the service was larger than Megan had expected, probably because of Jed's reputation in the investment community. Megan also suspected that some of the sympathizers dressed in somber black suits were no more than curious

sightseers who knew Jed slightly and had suddenly
become very interested in the rumors surrounding Jed McKearn and McKearn Investments. The
thought was a bitter pill, and behind the protection
of her dark veil, Megan's eyes narrowed with indignation.

With the passage of time, Anna McKearn was
beginning to accept the death of her husband. Aided
by her daughter's support and the kindness offered
by her widowed sister, Jessica, Anna was able to
compose herself during the brief ceremony at the
funeral parlor. However, standing now in the chill
air, staring down at the grave site, Anna's composure started to slip and she had to lean heavily upon
her sister's arm.

Megan whispered a silent prayer of thanks for
Aunt Jessica. She was a heavyset woman with taffy-
colored hair and her feet planted firmly on the
ground. She accepted everything life dealt her and
made the most of it. Common sense and a dry
humor had gotten her through several personal
crises of her own and were now helping Anna with
the trauma of widowhood.

Dry snowflakes had begun to fall from the heav-
ens, and a cold blast of wind blowing east from the
Rocky Mountains chilled the late-afternoon air with
the promise of winter. Brittle leaves swirled in the
gray skies before settling to earth and becoming
covered with a frigid mantle of white snow. The
somber wreaths collected powdery snow on their
fragile petals.

As Megan stood over the grave site, she let her

eyes wander past the family members to scan the interested faces in the crowd huddled nearby. How many people had come to pay their respects to Jedediah McKearn and how many were merely curious onlookers?

She forced her attention back to the preacher and berated herself for her cynicism. Too many days at the office fighting off reporters, dealing with worried account holders and fending off members of the board had given her a jaded outlook, she decided. Just as Garrett had suggested.

The fourth estate hadn't neglected Jed's funeral. The press was represented in full force, including reporters taking copious notes and photographers with their wide-angle lenses trained on the mourners. Megan recognized the hungry faces of the reporters who had been in her office on the day the story about the investment scam was given to the press by George Samples. Like vultures circling carrion, the reporters hovered near the crowd. Megan was bone tired, and it was all she could do to hold her tongue when Harold Dansen cast a baleful look in her direction.

Garrett stood on the fringes of the crowd, keeping his distance from Megan, just as he had on the day the story broke about the investment swindle. Though he was detached, his dark, probing eyes never left her face. Beneath the seclusion of her black veil, she could feel the intensity of his smoldering gaze. He stood slightly apart from the crowd, and though he was dressed only in a dark business suit, he didn't seem to notice the cold wind biting at his face and ruffling his thick, ebony hair. He looked as tired as she felt, and Megan had to force her gaze away from the weary angles of his face.

The funeral had been tiring. Megan was glad when the final prayer had been whispered and the coffin was lowered slowly into the brown earth. Her mother looked tired and pale when Megan took hold of her arm and maneuvered both Anna and Jessica toward the waiting limousine.

Megan managed to avoid members of the press as well as Garrett. Though she longed to be with him, she knew that she couldn't risk it. When her gaze locked silently with his for a heart-stopping instant, Megan was able to communicate to him without speaking, and he appeared to accept her unspoken request for privacy. He understood as well as she did the need for discretion. Already there was speculation that Megan and Garrett were romantically linked, and until the SEC investigation was complete, neither Megan nor Garrett could afford the adverse publicity their romance might engender.

As she reached the car, a heavy hand wrapped possessively around her forearm. Megan looked up, expecting to see Garrett. Instead, she was staring into the cold blue eyes of Ted Benson.

Megan forced a polite smile, which the lawyer returned. "I think we should talk," he suggested. "About Jed's will."

"Can it wait? Mom's tired and we expect a few guests to show up at the house."

Ted didn't expect that response. Nor did he like it. His thin lips pursed together tightly. "I suppose so. I could drop by in a few hours, after the crowd has thinned a little. We could talk then. Since you inherited Jed's share of the stock in McKearn Investments, we have a lot to discuss."

Megan hesitated. The day had already taken its toll on her mother. "I don't know. Tomorrow might be better—"

Ted frowned darkly. "I'm planning to go out of town tomorrow. Business. I'd like to start this ball rolling as soon as possible. Probate could be complicated."

"I'm not sure Mother's up to it," Megan hedged, casting a worried look at Anna, who had climbed into the limousine. Her head rested between the cushions and the shaded window, and her eyes were closed. Little lines of strain were visible on her otherwise flawless skin.

Ted sensed Megan's concern. "Then let me talk to you. Alone. We'll include your mother when I get back into town—the first part of next week." He paused dramatically. "There are a few other things we should discuss as well. Things that don't have anything to do with the will.

"The SEC investigation?"

"To start with."

Megan hazarded one last look at her mother. Aunt Jessica had slid into the car beside her sister and was patting Anna's hand affectionately. Anna managed a smile.

"What about now?" Ted suggested.

"I can't. I've got to go back to the house—"

"Let me drive you. We can talk on the way."

It seemed like the only solution to the problem. "Just a minute." She explained what was happening to her mother and Aunt Jessica, then reluctantly followed Ted Benson to his car.

Ted held the door open for her, and as she slid onto the plush leather seat, her eyes collided for a minute with the angry glare of Garrett Reaves. He was standing near his car and had watched the entire sequence of events between Ted Benson and Megan. The chilling look he sent her took Megan's breath away.

It was late by the time Megan convinced Ted to take her home. The afternoon at her mother's had been nearly as draining as the funeral itself. Ted Benson hadn't left her alone for a minute, and his insinuations about Garrett worried her. Ted seemed convinced that Garrett was involved in the scam and Megan found herself staunchly defending him. The thought of Garrett being linked to the scandal made her stomach turn, and she couldn't help but wonder if she'd been kidding herself about Garrett's innocence all along. She wanted so desperately to believe him.

Megan had expected Garrett to make an appearance at her mother's house. He hadn't. As each new guest had arrived to express condolences to the family, Megan had secretly hoped that Garrett would be the next. She had been disappointed.

Ted Benson had finished several drinks in the early evening and it became clear during the drive to Megan's apartment that he wanted to discuss more than her father's will. The digital clock on the dashboard of his Porsche quietly announced that it was nearly ten when he parked the car near the curb in front of her town house.

"Thanks for bringing me home," Megan whispered as she reached for the handle of the door. Ted wasn't deterred. He put a staying hand on Megan's sleeve.

"There are still things we should go over," he suggested, and his fingers crept up the soft leather of her coat.

"They'll keep," Megan replied.

"I'll be out of town."

"Then we'll discuss them when you get back. Maybe by then the investigation will be complete and everything will have calmed down a little."

"Don't kid yourself."

She opened the door.

The throbbing engine of the Porsche stopped as Ted extracted the key from the ignition. "Megan—"

The sound of her name as it sprang from Ted's lips was too familiar. His flirtations had gone much too far. She turned cold eyes toward him.

"Don't you think you should invite me in?" he asked suggestively, his thick white hair gleaming silver in the darkness.

"What I think, Ted, is that you should go home to your wife and children," she stated pointedly. Indignation sparked in her gray eyes.

"My children are grown and Eleanor and I have separated—"

"Not good enough, Ted." He looked as if she had slapped him. "In my book, married is married."

"Eleanor is going to file for divorce in a couple of

weeks. We're just working out the details. You understand."

But of course, she did. "Look, Ted, I don't think we should confuse our professional relationship."

"Who's confused?"

"You are," she said firmly. "Because that's all there is. You're the attorney for McKearn Investments. I'm the client. It's simple." Her words sounded cruel, but the last thing Megan wanted to do was lead the man on. He had earned both his reputations: as an excellent lawyer, and as a womanizer. Megan didn't want to give him even the slightest encouragement that she was interested in anything other than his professional services.

"So where do you get off—acting so pure?" he asked suddenly as he fumbled in the inner pocket of his jacket for his cigarettes. He shook one from the crumpled pack, and lit it with his gold lighter. The red ash glowed brightly in the dark interior of the car.

"I'm just telling you that I'm not interested—"

"These are the eighties. You're a free woman. You run the investment company, you're independently wealthy—or will be when Jed's estate is probated—"

"And I don't get involved with married men."

"Unless his name happens to be Garrett Reaves," Ted suggested. Megan stiffened. "I remember what happened between you and Reaves, Megan. You were seeing him when he was engaged to Lana Tremaine. At least, that's what your brother insisted." Ted took a long drag on the cigarette. "So don't act so damned virginal with me."

"Look, Ted, you're getting way out of line," Megan shot back. "I'll talk to you when you get back . . . about business!"

"You'd just better be careful," Ted warned, slurring his words slightly. "Reaves isn't the god you make him out to be."

"I don't—"

Ted waved off her protests. "Save it, Megan. You've defended him from the minute you found out about the scam."

"I'm just not sure that he's involved."

"Because you're too blind to see the truth. If Reaves were as innocent as you seem to think, why would he have Ron Thurston and his associates poking around, trying to find out everything there is to know about George Samples, McKearn Investments and you?"

Megan had begun to slide out of the car, but she stopped. What was Ted insinuating? Dread, like a clammy hand, began to climb up her spine. "What are you talking about?"

Ted smiled in satisfaction. "It seems Mr. Reaves is covering his bases. I wouldn't be surprised if he slapped you with a lawsuit for defamation of character or some such nonsense, just as a legal ploy."

"To put me on the defensive?" she whispered.

"To save his ass."

Megan tried to rise above the attorney's speculations. "How do you know all of this?"

Ted laughed and stubbed out his cigarette. "The legal community is pretty tight, or didn't you know that? Not much happens in this town that I don't know about. That's what your company pays me for.

Remember?" Carelessly he reached for her hand.
"Come on, Meg, lighten up. Ask me in and I'll let
you buy me a drink—"

"Go home, Ted," she said firmly, extracting her
hand. Then realizing how inebriated he had become,
she changed her mind. "Look, maybe you'd better
not drive. I'll call a cab."

"I could just stay here."

"Out of the question."

With her final rebuff, she shut the car door and
marched up the steps of her porch, intent on calling
a cab to retrieve him. It was too late. She heard Ted
swear loudly and start the engine of the flashy car.
Then the wide tires squealed and the engine roared
noisily into the night.

"Some men never grow up," she muttered to
herself as she unlocked the door and entered her
homey town house. Angrily she mounted the stairs;
she was still seething when she hung up her clothes
and slipped into her warm robe. Knowing she was
too restless to sleep, she went back downstairs and
made herself a warm cup of cocoa. She sipped the
creamy hot drink and smiled grimly. The hell with
calories. The hell with reporters. And the hell with
men like Ted Benson who thought they could charm
any woman into their bed.

Maybe that's my problem, she thought. *Maybe I
can't deal with the new morality.* Sleeping with a man
without commitment, quick one-night stands for
pure physical pleasure, weren't her style and never
had been. Sex was more than just a physical need; it
was an expression of mental attraction and compan-
ionship as well.

Then what about Garrett? He's never been committed to you! You're a hypocrite, Megan McKearn—saving yourself for the one man who has never done anything but use you. Ted Benson seemed to think Garrett was just using her again. She tried to ignore the lawyer's thoughts, dismissing them as idle conjecture from a tongue loosened by alcohol, but she couldn't. There was a thread of truth to Ted's convictions nagging at the back of her conscience.

The phone rang sharply. Megan nearly spilled the remainder of her hot chocolate at the sound. Despite the lingering suspicions in her mind, Megan prayed that Garrett would be on the other end of the line.

"Ms. McKearn?"

Megan's mouth turned into a frown of disappointment. "Yes."

"Harold Dansen. KRCY news." Though it was after ten at night, the tenacious reporter still had the audacity to call.

"Sorry to bother you . . . ," he apologized.

Then why did you? she thought angrily.

He was just getting to that. ". . . but I haven't been able to connect with you. Remember the other night at Diablo's? You promised me an interview," he wheedled.

"I haven't forgotten," Megan stated, biting her tongue to keep from giving him a piece of her tired mind. "It's just that I've been extremely busy."

"I know, and my condolences," Dansen interjected. "What about later in the week?"

"I don't know. My schedule is pretty full, and I don't have my appointment book with me. Could you call the office Monday morning and talk to my secretary, Jenny Hughs? Or better yet, I'll have her call you."

"I was hoping we could get together some time this weekend," he suggested.

Megan's voice was cool but polite. "I'm sorry, Mr. Dansen. My weekend is booked. If you could call the office Monday—"

"I tried that already." Megan could almost hear the smirk in his voice. Without words he was accusing her of avoiding him.

"Then let me call you next week after I've checked my schedule."

Knowing that he'd pushed as hard as he dared, Harold Dansen hung up the phone, determined to get to the bottom of the McKearn Investment fraud story *and* whatever other secrets Megan McKearn kept hidden.

When Megan placed the receiver back on the cradle of the phone, she let her hand linger on the cool, ivory-colored instrument. For a moment she considered calling Garrett, and then, realizing how late it was, decided against it. Besides which, she couldn't afford to be seen with him again. Since her father's death, Megan had been under more scrutiny than she ever would have imagined.

The press had refused to leave her alone. The phone hadn't stopped ringing since the day Jed passed away. Even though her number was unlisted, the press had gotten hold of it. Megan suspected that George Samples had eagerly provided the news media with her personal number and address. Changing telephone numbers hadn't been difficult, but she didn't relish the idea of moving. At least not yet. She didn't have the time or the energy. Megan took another sip of her now cool cocoa and frowned.

Somehow, Harold Dansen had gotten hold of her new phone number. It wouldn't be long before the rest of the media would have it as well. With a sigh, she drained her hot chocolate, licked her lips and walked into the kitchen. After setting her empty cup in the sink, she started up the stairs. When she was on the third step, the doorbell chimed and Megan bristled.

Who would be calling on her at this hour of night? The most probable person was Ted Benson. No doubt he had stopped at a local bar for a nightcap on the way home and with renewed fortification was approaching her once again. This time she would make her position undeniably clear, even if it meant she would have to hire another lawyer to handle the legal work for McKearn Investments.

When Garrett watched Megan leave the cemetery with Ted Benson, his jaw hardened and his back teeth pressed together uncomfortably. Jealousy swept over him in a hot wave. He was able to hide his anger by pushing his fists deep into his pockets and avoiding eye contact with any of the lingering mourners. But the sense of vengeful jealousy overtaking him made his dark eyes glower ominously.

Common sense told him he couldn't cause a scene, but a primal urge akin to possession clouded his judgment. Only after several minutes of wrathful deliberation did he decide to bide his time . . . until he was certain to corner Megan alone.

And now, many hours later, the waiting was over.

He'd given Megan more than enough time to return to her apartment. It was nearly eleven when he finally called and the monotonous beep of a busy signal told him Megan was home.

It took him less than ten minutes to drive from the bar to her apartment. After hours of quietly sipping a beer and disinterestedly watching cable sports, he was anxious to reach her. He parked the car less than a block from her building and strode meaningfully to her door.

Tonight he had a plan. After three years of excuses and lies, he was done with all the indirect messages and vague insinuations, the usual crap that happened between a man and a woman. Tonight he was interested only in the truth and one woman. And he intended to have both.

He rang the bell impatiently. Within seconds, Megan peeked through the window, recognized him and opened the door. Her smile was tight and there was a new wariness in her stance as she leaned against the door and watched him through eyes narrowed in undisguised suspicion.

Garrett heard the door close softly behind him. He stood in the hallway, his hands thrust into the pockets of the same suit pants he had worn all day. When he turned to face her, he noticed that she hadn't moved. Her arms were folded beneath her breasts, and one shoulder was pressed against the wooden door for support.

"Pack an overnight bag. You're coming with me," he announced without any trace of a smile.

Megan stood stock-still. It was evident that

Garrett was angry, but he was shouting orders to her as if he'd lost his mind.

"Wait a minute . . ."

"I said, get some clothes together," Garrett instructed, his voice low and commanding.

"Why?"

"I told you. I want you to spend the weekend with me."

Her elegant eyebrows arched expressively. "Did it ever occur to you to ask?"

"Look, Megan, I'm tired of all the double-talk. I want you to come to Boulder for the weekend. I've waited all day for you, and I'm sick of worrying about your reputation, the lawsuit, the past and all the other ridiculous excuses we've used to avoid the real issue!" he exclaimed, his voice rising with the intensity of his words.

"And I'm tired of men trying to manipulate me." A thin smile curved her lips, and she shook her head as if she couldn't believe what she was hearing. Her coppery hair glinted in golden streaks as it swept against the plush velour of her robe. For a moment, Garrett was tempted to forget everything but making love to her long into the night. Angry color gave her cheeks a rosy hue, and her round eyes seemed silvery in the dim light of the room.

"The only people who are manipulated are those who let someone else run their lives."

"Then you'll understand why I think we should forget about spending the weekend together."

"Don't do it, Megan," he warned, the skin tightening over the angular planes of his face. He pointed an unsteady finger at her face. "What I understand is that there is only one *real* issue here."

"And that is?"

"That either we care for each other, or everything we've shared isn't worth a plug nickel. Do we have something special, or is this whole . . . relationship built on lies? It is real or is it a lot of bull?" He flipped his wrist upward in an impatient gesture of annoyance and then slapped the wall near the door with his rigid hand. "Damn it, Megan, just what the hell are we doing to each other?" he asked in a lower, more cautious voice. His broad shoulders sagged, as if the burden were suddenly too much to bear.

Garrett was leaning against the wall, only a few feet from her, and yet she felt that the wide abyss separating them could never be bridged. Could she ever learn to trust him? Could she take the chance? Was the prize worth the risk?

The emotional day had taken its toll on her, and she felt an uncomfortable lump forming in her throat. Garrett straightened his shoulders and pulled angrily at the knot in his tie. The lines near his eyes were deep, evidence of the strain robbing him of slumber.

Despite her earlier doubts, Megan felt her heart bleed for this man. She touched him gently on the cheek, and the tips of her fingers encountered the rough hairs of his beard. Garrett closed his eyes and groaned as if in physical pain.

"Why don't you stay here," she suggested. "We've both been through a lot. You're tired . . ."

"Of people who don't know what they want." His

eyes opened quickly, and he pushed aside the seduction of her hand. "If I stay here tonight, nothing really will change. It's too convenient. When I'm in the city, I spend the night." He shook his dark head and scowled. His eyes pierced into her soul. "I want more."

"I don't understand—"

"You're not trying." His hazel eyes flashed savagely. "Casual nights aren't enough."

"And you think a weekend in Boulder will be?"

His dark gaze slid downward from her mysterious eyes, past her parted lips, the column of her throat, the curve of her breasts to linger on the sash holding her bathrobe closed. He wanted her as desperately as he ever had, and the heat in his loins throbbed mercilessly. He shifted uncomfortably.

"I don't know if there is enough," he admitted in a hoarse whisper, and forced his gaze back to her face.

Megan's lips pulled into a wistful frown. "You really have no right, you know," she said calmly. "No right to come barging in here and making demands on me."

"Are you coming with me or not?"

It was an ultimatum—pure and simple. She had no doubt that if he left tonight he would never be back. But there was more to it than that. In his own way, he was reaching out to her. . . . The decision was easy.

"It will only take me a minute to pack."

Chapter Nine

ʃilence and darkness.

The interior of the car was shadowed, and the only sound to disturb the stillness of the night was the whine of the engine as the sporty vehicle headed toward Garrett's remote mountain home. Headlights pierced through the darkness and reflected on the large snowflakes falling from the dark sky and beginning to cover the little-used country road.

The tension inside the BMW was so charged that Megan's stomach had tightened into painful knots. Her fingers drummed restlessly on the armrest. Garrett was near enough that she could have touched him with the slightest of movements. She didn't. When she chanced a secretive glance in his direction, she noticed that the square angle of his jaw was set in a hard line of determination. He looked like a man hell-bent to get accomplished whatever task he set for himself.

Disturbing thoughts flitted through Megan's tired mind, creating a small, dull headache behind her eyes. Had Ted Benson been right after all? Was Garrett setting Megan up just to watch her fall? She closed her eyes against the thought that, just possibly, Garrett was desperate and ruthless enough to use her fragile relationship with him as a weapon in the courtroom battle he had promised. Ted Benson had assured her that Garrett planned to sue McKearn Investments. According to Benson, it was only a matter of time before Garrett played his trump card and sought revenge against McKearn Investments.

As he drove, Garrett's eyes never left the slick pavement winding through the foothills. He concentrated on holding the sporty car on the road. Several times the tires of the BMW spun wildly against the snow-covered pavement and he silently cursed himself for not bringing the Bronco. The accumulation of snow made driving more hazardous than he had predicted, and his hands grasped the steering wheel in a death grip. He attempted to keep his mind on driving and off the gentle curve of Megan's knee, which his fingers sometimes brushed when he shifted gears. Even though she was wearing heavy winter clothes, she was the most damnably seductive woman he had ever met.

Megan sat nervously in the passenger seat. Occasionally she would let her gaze wander surreptitiously to the tense features on Garrett's face, but for the most part she, too, stared out of the window and waited to see what the night, and the enigmatic man sitting next to her, would bring.

The strain of the forced silence finally got to her. She had expected an explanation from Garrett, but when, after nearly a half hour, he hadn't spoken, she decided to take the bull by the horns and get to the bottom of his unspoken hostility.

"Why was it so important that I come with you tonight?" she finally asked, tilting her head to face him.

"I told you, I'm tired of playing games."

"Is that what we were doing?"

"You were avoiding me."

"Oh, Garrett." Her words were expelled in a weary sigh. "I was only being cautious." For the first time she realized just how tired he looked. His hair was unruly, his face nearly gaunt with lines of worry. How many sleepless nights had he spent recently, and why?

"Tonight, lady, we're going to work this out," he promised as a tiny muscle worked angrily in his jaw. The car slid on an upgrade, and with a curse, Garrett downshifted. His fingers grazed her knee, causing Megan's heart to trip.

She lifted her shoulders in a dismissive gesture that belied her turmoil of inner emotions and concern for him, then turned to stare out the window once again.

The rest of the drive was accomplished in silence, and Megan was relieved to see the dark silhouette of Garrett's house when the car slid around the final curve in the road.

Once Garrett had parked the car, he opened the door for Megan and hoisted her small valise from the back seat. The stone manor, tucked sedately in the snow-laden pines, seemed slightly forbidding. The windows were dark and the panes covered with a thin layer of ice. Snow piled on the flatter surfaces of the roof, to glisten in the ethereal illumination of the security lights near the garage.

Frigid air brushed over Megan's face and snowflakes clung tenaciously to her hair. Involuntarily, she shivered as Garrett unlocked the heavy wooden door and stepped aside to let her enter.

The interior of the Tudor home was as cold as the night. When Garrett flipped on the lights and adjusted the thermostat, Megan tried not to stare at the disheveled state of the rustic old house. Very obviously something was wrong here.

The carpets were rolled and bound. The warm wood floors were covered with a thin layer of dust and most of the furniture had been draped with heavy sheets. Clothes, books and various memorabilia were scattered haphazardly around the rooms branching from the foyer.

Only the den looked as if anyone had cared enough to keep it clean and comfortable.

Garrett noticed Megan's confused look as she stared at the disarray in the beautiful old house. "Maid's day off," he joked bitterly.

"Not funny, Garrett. What happened?"

"I'm living in the apartment in Denver," he responded with a disinterested lift of his broad shoulders. He kneeled before the stone fireplace and began arranging kindling as if to start a fire. His actions said more clearly than words, *end of discussion.*

Megan wouldn't be put off. After all, *he* was the one who had dragged her here. "But I don't understand," she whispered, her eyes roving restlessly over the pine walls. Distractedly she ran a finger along the bookcase and then brushed the dust on her jeans. "I thought you liked living here."

"I did." The fire ignited and began to crackle against the pitchy wood. Garrett stared into the golden flames.

"Then why?"

"It was something you said," he stated, rising from his kneeling position on the hearth and dusting his hands together. "Something about too many ghosts from the past." His hazel eyes touched hers for a moment, and then, obviously uncomfortable, he dismissed the difficult subject. "You look like you could use a cup of hot coffee," he decided. "I'll be right back." After flashing her what was intended to be his most charming smile, he walked out of the room.

He looks older than he should, Megan decided. Had guilt over the investment scam and worry about being found out aged him?

Megan tightened the ribbon holding her hair and shook off the uneasy thoughts. She considered offering to help him with the coffee, but decided to wait and see what the evening had in store for her. This was Garrett's idea; let him show his hand. For someone who wasn't interested in playing games, he was doing a damned good job of keeping Megan in the dark.

In the short time that Garrett was gone, Megan fidgeted and studied the interior of the home he had so dearly loved. Why would he move?

Memories of the fateful night three years ago assailed her senses and crowded her mind. A wistful smile caressed her lips as she remembered the touch of his fingers as they'd softly caressed her skin, the taste of his lips as they'd whispered softly over hers, the feel of his muscles, strident and lean, as they'd pressed urgently against her body. The powerful images, as fresh as if they had happened yesterday, reawakened feelings for Garrett she had hoped would die.

Even though she had been with him once since that tragic night, Megan wasn't sure of herself. Nor did she know where her feelings of love might lead. The future appeared as stormy as the past.

Tears threatened to spill, but she valiantly held them at bay. Perhaps it was better to forget what she and Garrett had shared. . . .

Megan gritted her teeth against the familiar feelings of love that began to fill her mind. She shivered from the cold, and though the fire took hold and the hungry orange flames began to give off a little warmth, she still sat huddled on the hearth, dressed only in the faded pair of jeans, bulky ski sweater, thick parka and boots she had hurriedly donned when Garrett insisted that she come with him.

"It'll warm up soon," Garrett solemnly predicted as he walked back into the room and noticed her chattering teeth. He was carrying two steaming mugs. The welcome fragrance of coffee scented the air. Garrett hesitated at the bar. He reached for a bottle of scotch, read the label, frowned and replaced it. "Can I get you anything else?"

Eyeing the liquor dubiously, she shook her head. "I don't think so." The heat from the fire was beginning to touch her back, and for the first time since leaving her apartment she was beginning to feel warm. "The only thing I want from you tonight is an explanation."

"For?"

"Cut it out, Garrett. You're the one who doesn't want to play games. Remember?" She pushed her palms on her thighs, rose to her full height, picked up her cup and walked toward the window. "Why don't you explain to me why, all of a sudden, in the middle of the night, it was so bloody important to shanghai me here."

His thick brows lifted expressively. "You came of your own volition," he pointed out. Her mouth quirked downward but she refrained from protesting. "That, at least, is encouraging," he muttered under his breath.

Forgetting his earlier decision to abstain, he grabbed a bottle of brandy and splashed some of the amber liquor into his mug before lifting the bottle in a gesture of offering. Megan frowned and shook her head. Tonight she didn't want any alcohol to cloud her judgment. She couldn't afford to replay the tragic scene from her past.

"Why did you bring me here?"

"I want to talk to you."

"About the SEC investigation," she guessed.

"Among other things."

"You and half the population of Colorado—"

"What's that supposed to mean?"

"Only that my phone hasn't stopped ringing for the past two weeks." She stared into the knowing eyes of the only man she had ever loved. *When would it end?*

He smiled mysteriously. "Then maybe it's a good thing that you came here tonight. At least you won't be subjected to the phone for the rest of the weekend . . . and you and I won't be interrupted." A gleam of smoky satisfaction lighted his eyes as he took a long swallow of the scalding liquid and observed her over the rim of his cup. His thick, black hair curled in unruly waves over his ears. Had it not been for the lines of worry on his face and the cynicism tainting his charming smile, he would have been as ruggedly handsome as he had ever been.

The hard angle of his jaw relaxed slightly, and Megan felt all her earlier hostilities dissipating into the cold mountain night. The hint of a bemused smile tugged at the corners of his mouth.

"I talked to Ted Benson today," she said, and took a sip of her coffee. It burned the back of her throat.

"I noticed." The smile faded. Garrett was suddenly wary.

"He seems to think that you plan on dropping a lawsuit in my lap."

Garret studied the delicate contours of her face. "Why?"

She shrugged. "Rumor, I guess. He insinuated that you asked your attorney to find all the skeletons in my family closet."

"That doesn't make too much sense, does it?" he scoffed, but despite his feigned nonchalance there was an involuntary tensing of his muscles.

"Why not?"

Because I already know about them all—I was there the night Patrick died."

A suffocating silence settled in the room. Megan stared into the black depths of her coffee before taking a seat near the fire. "What's that supposed to mean?"

"The only skeletons I'm concerned with are those that keep pushing you away from me. That night, three years ago, started all the trouble between us. And if we're ever . . . going to rise above what happened, we'll have to understand it first."

"I don't see any reason to dredge up the past." She looked away from his probing stare.

"I do." His voice was cold and determined. "You still blame me for Patrick's death . . . and I want to know why." The frustrations of three painful years contorted his face. "For God's sake, Megan, I barely knew your brother."

"You've got it all wrong," she whispered, forcing herself to meet his dark, uncompromising gaze. "It's not you I blame." She closed her eyes against the torture of the truth.

"But I thought—"

She silenced him by raising a trembling palm. "If anyone's to blame . . . I am." Her voice was barely audible.

He was stunned. *"Why?"*

She set her cup on the flagstone hearth and wrapped her arms around her knees. The secret she had hidden from Garrett in the past came reluctantly to her lips. "Patrick told me that you were engaged." Garrett frowned, but didn't interrupt. "Earlier that day he had shown me the proof—and article torn out of a paper—the engagement announcement. He thought you were using me."

"And you believed him." Garrett's face had twisted into a mask of disgust.

"Of course not!" Megan sighed wearily and fought against the tears that always threatened when she thought of that one painful night. Images of Patrick's boyish face, contorted in condemnation and self-righteousness, flashed through her mind. He had tried to help her—hoped to warn her about Garrett—and she, in her own stubborn, prideful way, hadn't listened. "I told him that you wouldn't use me, and to prove it to myself I came back here . . . to meet you . . ." Her voice faded, and a shiver as cold as the winter snow ran down her spine. Garrett sat down next to her and silently brushed a tear from her eye.

"Oh, Megan," he moaned, remembering her innocence and vulnerability. It was his fault, he told himself. He had pushed her into something she wasn't able to accept. He had known that Megan had been distracted earlier that evening, but he hadn't been able to guess the reason for her unease. And he hadn't been able to coerce her into telling him what was bothering her. He had tried to comfort her, and Megan had responded willingly. Her surrender had been complete, and he had thought that the tears in her eyes as his body had claimed hers were tears of selfless love. He had trusted her completely for those few intimate hours—until the morning newspaper had callously announced to the world that Patrick McKearn, only son of a wealthy Denver businessman had been killed in a single-car accident. The other passenger in the car was dead as well. Garrett closed his eyes against the memory of Megan's tortured face when she had read the article and flung the offensive paper across the room.

"No!" she had screamed, refusing to believe that her only brother was dead.

"I didn't believe Patrick," Megan said, swallowing against the dryness that had settled in her throat. Her gray eyes beseeched him. "I was so convinced that you weren't involved with anyone else that I didn't mention my argument with Patrick to you. I thought if I brought it up it would seem as if I doubted you."

"And you did." After three years, he finally understood the wariness in her eyes when he had first made love to her.

"No!" she nearly shouted, before lowering her quavering voice. "At least not then."

"But later?"

"Garrett, you *married* Lana."

"On the rebound, Megan. You wouldn't see me," he reminded her.

"Because of the guilt, damn it!" she said in an explosive burst of anger. "While you and I were here, in this very room, drinking imported champagne and making love, Patrick was trying to reach me!" The tears began in earnest, flowing down her cheeks in hot rivulets of grief and frustration.

"What does that have to do with anything?"

Garrett asked, placing a comforting hand on her shoulder. Quickly Megan stood, breaking the physical contact between them.

"Patrick was in trouble that night. He knew it and he tried to reach me—"

"Didn't he know you were with me?"

She shook her head, and her hair, still damp from the melting snowflakes, glistened in the fireglow. "He thought we'd broken up. He assumed that, after I cooled off, I would come to my senses and believe the newspaper article he'd given me."

Garrett wasn't convinced. "He could have guessed that you were here."

Her gray eyes pierced into his. "Don't you remember, Garrett? We took the phone off the hook so as not to be disturbed." Megan rubbed her temple with her fingers, trying to relieve the pressure building behind her eyes. "He was probably looking for me when the accident occurred."

"You don't know that."

"But I have to live with it. Every day of my life."

"You can't blame yourself."

She smiled grimly. "Funny. That's what I've told myself, over and over. I guess I'm just not very convincing."

Garrett was trying to make some sense out of what she was saying. "You said that Patrick was in trouble. What kind of trouble?"

Megan hesitated, sure that she had divulged too much already. Garrett seemed sincere, and in her heart she felt she could trust him with her most intimate secret . . . And yet, he had betrayed her in the past and had reason to lie to her now.

Garrett read the doubts clouding her normally clear gaze. He ran tense fingers through his hair and tried to think straight. How much of what she was saying was true, and how much was the result of three burdened years of guilt? He damned himself for the brandy clouding his mind.

But was it the liquor or the woman? He didn't seem to think clearly whenever she was near him, and he had vowed that tonight he would have all the answers to the questions that had been plaguing him for three long years. It was his move.

"I had been engaged to Lana," Garrett admitted. He finished his coffee and tossed the dregs into the fire. The flames sputtered noisily as he collected his ragged thoughts. "But I thought it was over. Honestly, Megan, you have to believe that. I just hadn't gotten around to making an official announcement. I wanted to give Lana the time to handle it her own way."

"It doesn't matter," she lied.

"Of course it does." When he stood, he reached for her, and this time she didn't pull away from him. "As long as there is anything or anyone standing between us, it matters." He folded her into the strength of his arms, holding her in an unwavering embrace. "Now, tell me, when Patrick tried to get hold of you . . . what happened?"

Her face contorted with pain. "Don't you remember?"

"What I remember is that I spent the night here, right in front of this fireplace, with the most beautiful woman I've ever had the misfortune to meet."

Megan managed a thin smile, and he touched her

chin with his finger. When she looked into his eyes, she felt as if she could die in their warm, hazel depths.

"It was a wonderful night, Megan . . . ," he murmured against her hair. Her pulse jumped and her heart throbbed painfully in her chest.

Garrett kissed her softly on the forehead, his lips warm and familiar against her skin.

"It was the night Patrick was killed," she said dully, all her beautiful memories shattered by that one last, tragic fact. She slipped away from the tenderness of his embrace and wrapped her arms around herself as if experiencing a sudden chill. It was so like the last time she was here. The cold promise of winter, the inviting crackle of the fire, the warmth of Garrett's arms. She stared sightlessly out the window.

"Megan." His voice was low and filled with pain. "I want to hear the rest of what happened that night."

"I'm sure you read about it—"

"The press may have exaggerated, or been paid to cover up some of the facts."

"By whom?"

"Who do you think? Your father was a pretty influential man. If he wanted to, he could have bought any of the reporters—"

"*If* he'd wanted to, and *if* he'd found someone dishonest enough to distort the facts."

"Everybody has a price."

"Do they, Garrett?" she asked with a glance in his direction. "And what's yours? What would *you* pay to keep your name out of the mud?" Then, when he didn't immediately respond, she turned her back to him and thought aloud, "Just how far would you go? For example, would you be willing to leak a little inside information on your company to a broker, so that he could let some other investors make money on a few well-placed trades?"

"Of course not!"

She turned to face him, disguising the fact that her heart was beating with dread. Tense lines of strain webbed from his eyes and bracketed his mouth. "But that's exactly what happened last April."

His eyes glittered dangerously. "If anyone—other than myself—made money selling short on Reaves Chemical stock, it was because of George Samples. It had nothing to do with me, Megan."

She wanted to believe him, but a trace of doubt still remained. "Then why would George take the chance and let your account become involved with his scam?"

Garrett shook his head. "I don't know."

"It just doesn't make much sense," she whispered as her secret fears mounted. With a sigh, she dropped into the corner of the couch, pulled off her boots, tucked her feet beneath her and rested her head against the leather cushions. It had been a long, grueling day, and she was exhausted.

Garrett shook his head in bewilderment and swore softly. He had been studying this same puzzle for weeks. He felt sure the answer was within his grasp—if only he could find it. "I was hoping that by now this entire mess would be behind us. I thought the SEC would have nailed the culprits and exposed whoever it was over at the newspaper who helped George with his scam."

"It takes time."

"Maybe not." Garrett's eyes suddenly sparked. "If I know Samples, he'll talk. He's not about to take the rap himself. Right now he's got a few of his friends involved with him, and so far, no one is rocking the boat."

"Except you."

"Exactly. So who's he covering for? Someone who works at the newspaper."

"Or . . . someone who does research for the *Denver Financial Times*," Megan surmised. "It could be anyone attached to the paper, not necessarily a reporter."

"What about the columns? Were they written by the same person?" He placed his hands on his thighs and sat next to her on the couch.

Megan shook her head. "I don't know, but I don't think so. If only one reporter were involved, it would be too obvious and the SEC would have already found him out."

"Maybe they have," Garrett said cryptically. "Maybe the government is just waiting until all the evidence is compiled before they act."

"It could take months. Anyone could have been working with George. A reporter, a delivery boy, a secretary, even a janitor—anyone who had access to the offices and knew where to look could have called George before the stories were printed." Garrett was listening to her intently, and he tugged thoughtfully on his lower lip.

Megan saw a glimmer of secret knowledge flicker in his eyes. "Wait a minute—you've figured something out, haven't you?"

"I'm not really sure," he evaded, stretching his arms and clasping them behind his head. "But, dear lady, I think that I'm about to be cleared in this swindle."

"You think you know who George's accomplice is," Megan surmised with a quick intake of breath. Was it possible that Garrett really wasn't involved in the scam and that he was just as desperate as she to find the culprits responsible for the scandal? Her heart missed a beat in anticipation.

"A theory."

"Which you have no intention of sharing with me."

Garrett's easy smile slanted across his face. "Not yet. As I said, it's only a theory."

"No proof to back it up." Megan's fingers tapped nervously on the arm of the couch as her mind worked in crazy circles. Who? Who would be involved with George, worked for the *Denver Financial Times,* and was clever enough to avoid suspicion? It was obvious from the satisfied smile on Garrett's face that he thought he knew the answer. His eyes had taken on a ruthless, vengeful gleam.

A comfortable silence settled between them, and Garrett placed his arm around her shoulders. "I've missed you," he admitted raggedly.

She laughed at the irony of the situation. "I've missed you, too."

The arm across her shoulders tightened and drew her close to him. "We've been through a lot, you and

I, together and apart. I'd like to think that we can face whatever happens in the future together."

She swallowed with difficulty. Anticipation mingled with dread. "Together?"

"I've done a lot of thinking, Megan. After your father died and it was nearly impossible to see you, I decided that it would be best if we made a clean break. You go your way and I go mine. I even went so far as to move out of this house and talk to a real estate broker about selling it."

Megan closed her eyes. *A clean break from Garrett.* Now that she had been with him again, would she be able to survive without him? She braced herself against his brutal rejection. Not only was he pushing *her* aside, but this beautiful old house as well. "But you haven't . . . put the house on the market?"

"I couldn't."

"Why not?" she whispered, barely able to breathe.

"The ghosts are here for me, too," he conceded. "But I'm not afraid of them. In fact—"he placed a strong finger under her chin and tipped her face upward to meet the conviction of his gaze"—I like the memories we shared here. Selling this place would be like cutting out a very important part of my life—a part I would rather keep."

Her lips trembled as they parted. Slowly he lowered his face and covered her mouth with his. Strong fingers twined in her hair and cradled her head against his. Her pulse began to race wildly as hot, insatiable urges uncoiled within her. Her fears fled as he slowly untied the ribbon holding her hair away from her face. The auburn curls tumbled free of their bond in tangled disarray.

"Garrett, please," she whispered, surrendering herself to the heat of his passion. His tongue slid between her teeth to savor the sweet moistness of her mouth and flick with lightning swiftness against its mate. Megan responded with a compliant moan.

He unzipped her parka, slid it off her shoulders and tossed it onto the floor. His warm fingers found the hem of her sweater and slowly discovered the supple muscles of her back. His hand splayed possessively over her spine to inch slowly upward, tracing each of her ribs with an exploring finger.

Megan's hands released the buttons of his shirt and touched the rock-hard muscles of his chest. With an impatient movement he jerked off the cotton garment and tossed it recklessly onto the floor near her parka.

His eyes glittered savagely as she moved first one hand and then the other against the soft mat of black hair covering his bronzed skin. The muscles of his chest flexed when one of her fingers toyed with his nipple; he was forced to close his eyes against the sweet agony.

"You're wanton," he whispered as his mouth brushed her eyelids.

"Only with you."

His entire body became rigid, and his eyes drilled into hers. "Don't lie to me, Megan," he warned. His hand moved upward, and he felt the weight of her breast in his palm.

She moaned softly as his fingers moved in slow, delicious circles near her nipple and she began to ache with the want of him. "I've . . . never lied to you, Garrett," she murmured, disappointment crossing her face when he removed his hands.

"Maybe not," he decided, lifting his body away from her and capturing her wrists between the steel-like fingers of one hand. "But you've certainly evaded the truth."

Her chin inched defiantly upward. "I can't say that I've never been interested in another man," she admitted, filled with fierce pride and outrage. "And I really don't care if you believe me or not. But the fact of the matter is that I've never had the urge to become intimate with anyone."

He snorted his disbelief. "You've never slept with another man?"

"It's none of your business, Garrett. That was your decision."

His jaw tensed in frustration. "You can't expect me to believe you were faithful to me."

"I don't give a damn what you believe!" she lied, and smiled cynically. "I don't subscribe to the double standard, you know. And as far as being faithful, I didn't intend to be. You were married, for God's sake! I didn't feel I owed you any fidelity whatsoever."

He cocked an interested eyebrow, begging her to continue.

"But . . . it just didn't happen," she said slowly.

She expected him to be relieved, but the expression on his rugged features was one of torment and self-disgust as he gazed down on her. Slowly he released her wrists. "I never meant to hurt you, Megan," he insisted, wrapping his arms around her

shoulders and pushing a wayward strand of hair from
her eyes. "I've always loved you." It was a reluctant
admission, and Megan would have willingly given
her soul to believe him. If it hadn't been for his brief
marriage, she might have trusted the honesty in his
eyes and the pain in the tight corners of his mouth.
As it was, she accepted what he said as an easy
excuse brought on by the heat of the moment.

Her fingers ran through his wavy dark hair, and
her eyes filled with the love she had always felt for
him. "Just love me tonight, darling," she whispered,
forcing his head down and touching the tip of his
nose with her lips.

He responded by pressing his lips ruthlessly
against hers and plundering her mouth with the
supple grace of his tongue. She tasted the sweet
maleness of him and returned his passion with all of
the heat welling in her body. Her heart pounded
wildly within the prison of her chest.

He slid her sweater over her head and watched in
satisfaction when she shook her hair free and it
tumbled in coppery splendor against the soft white
skin of her shoulders. The ivory-colored bra hid
nothing from his knowing eyes. Her breasts heaved
against the lacy fabric, and the dark nipples formed
shadowy peaks that invited his touch. He outlined
first one and then the other of the nipples with his
tongue, moistening the sheer fabric before removing
the soft barrier between his mouth and the aching
sweetness.

When he captured one taut nipple in his mouth,
his hands gripped Megan's shoulders and he re-

versed their positions. She was atop him, her hair falling forward and whispering against his chest in featherlight strokes. He groaned as he pushed against Megan's back, forcing her rosy nipple once again into the warm cavern of his mouth. Megan felt his teeth against her, nibbling and teasing her with expert prowess. She sighed convulsively when he began to suckle.

"Dear God," she whispered, her blood pounding dizzyingly against her temples.

One of his hands slipped between her jeans and the soft skin of her abdomen. Involuntarily, she sucked in her breath, allowing him the freedom to touch all of her. She felt the zipper slide and the pants being pushed down until the chill of the night touched her skin.

Garrett moved out from under her and stood next to the couch. Bereft of his touch, she watched through the veil of thick lashes while he slowly, sensuously, unbuckled his belt. It slid through the loops to fall to the floor. Her eyes caught his for an instant, then dropped once again to his hips, watching while he lazily stepped out of his pants.

He stood naked before her, his lean, corded muscles flexed with the restraint he was demanding of his body. Beads of frustrated sweat clung to his forehead. He bent to turn off the one lamp that remained, and she caught a glimpse of the fluid muscles of his shoulders sliding against each other before the room was suddenly dark, illuminated only by the scarlet shadows of a dying fire.

"I want you," he said, still keeping the few inches

of space between them. "But more than that, I want to know that what we share won't be just for one night."

She smiled mysteriously, reached for his hand and pulled on his arm, forcing his body closer to hers. "I've wanted to hear those words for a long time," she admitted as he leaned over and kissed her cheeks. "Love me, Garrett."

"I always have." With his final vow, he gently pressed his weight against her and covered her lips with his. The heat within him became unbound, and desire, molten hot, surged through his veins.

She felt his rippling muscles straining against hers, moving in the gentle rhythm of love. One knee parted her legs and she willingly arched against him, anxious to have the burning ache within her salved by his gentle movements.

Her breathing was shallow and rapid, and a thin sheen of perspiration covered her body. Her fingers dug into the firm muscles of his shoulders until, persuaded that she needed him as desperately as he wanted her, Garrett kissed her fiercely at the moment his body found hers.

He pushed her into a faster tempo of love, pulsating with the liquid fire running in his veins, until they exploded as one, coming together in a union of flesh that was as savage as it was tender. The stillness of the mountain night was shattered by Megan's impassioned cry of love. Her breathing was ragged, and for a moment she thought her heart would burst with the passionate love she harbored for this one man.

Tenderly he pushed her hair out of her eyes,

letting his fingers linger against her wet skin. "Sweet lady," Garrett whispered lovingly, "I need you."

Megan swallowed against the lump forming in her throat. Firelight reflected in his intense gaze. "And I need you, love," she murmured, blinking back the tears of happiness pooling in her eyes.

Chapter Ten

𝒢et up, lazybones."

Garrett's familiar voice pierced into her subconscious and slowly dragged Megan out of her dreamed-filled sleep. As consciousness returned she realized that she had spent the final few hours of the night making passionate love to the man she loved. A happy smile tugged at the corners of her mouth as she stretched.

After opening an experimental eyelid, she curled into a ball and hiked the bedcovers around her neck. "Wake me when it's morning," she grumbled goodnaturedly, and rolled over intending to get a few more hours of desperately needed sleep.

"That will be a while." Garrett made a dramatic show of checking his watch. "About twenty hours, as a matter of fact. It's nearly noon now."

"Just a few more minutes—"

"Not on your life." He gave her rump a sound pat, and she groaned as she rolled over to face him, clutching the pale blue sheet over her naked breasts. The look she sent him could have melted stone.

He laughed at her consternation. "I didn't bring you up here just so you could spend the day in bed."

She cocked a disbelieving eyebrow. "You could have fooled me," she teased, a seductive light glinting in her gray eyes. Her dark hair tumbled freely around her face and she licked her lips provocatively as she stared up at him.

Garrett's eyes flicked over her body with obvious interest. "If you don't get up now, you may never again get the chance," he warned with a cynical smile.

"Promises . . . promises." With a petulant frown, she started to rise, but Garrett was beside her in an instant, stripping off his clothes in disgust.

"You seductive little witch," he muttered. "You're making me crazy."

"And you love it," she laughed, raising the sheet as he slid into the bed next to her. His fingers caught in her thick, unruly auburn curls.

"What I love, lady, is to spend time with you." He shifted his weight over her and pressed anxious, hungry lips to hers. "You're a tease . . . a beautiful, wanton, wicked tease."

His hard, lean body rubbed sensuously against the silkiness of her skin, and his eyes darkened with the desire only she could inflame. Never had Megan looked more beautiful. Never had Garrett wanted her more. His body ached with the need of her, and he wondered, as his lips found the hollow of her throat, if he would ever get enough of her.

After a hearty breakfast, Garrett insisted that Megan follow him to the stables. Despite her teasing protests, he saddled two of his three horses and helped a laughing Megan into the saddle.

The remainder of the afternoon was spent horseback riding through the thick stands of pine and aspen surrounding the estate. A wintry afternoon sun glistened against the snow covering the ground.

The horses' breaths misted in the cold mountain air as the animals followed an overgrown path through the woods. Garrett explained that when he stayed in the city, a neighbor, Sam Jordan, took care of the animals and had offered to buy all of them if Garrett decided to go through with his plan to sell the mountain retreat.

Just the thought of Garrett giving up the house that he so obviously loved saddened Megan. "You can't sell the horses," she complained, bending forward in the saddle and patting Mariah's thick, dark neck. The horse snorted her agreement and tossed her black head in the air, jingling the bridle.

Garrett sat astride Cody, a large buckskin gelding who swished his black tail impatiently and flattened his ears against his head as if he knew he was the center of attention. "I don't want to," Garrett admitted, casting Megan a rueful glance. "But it's not that easy commuting to Denver in the winter."

"You've got the four-wheel drive and an apartment in the city in case you get stranded or have to stay overnight." Megan frowned and bit on her lower lip. "Looks to me like you have the best of both worlds . . . besides which, you love it here. You could never sell it to a stranger."

Garrett let out his breath and didn't immediately respond. He guided Cody along the seldom-used path that twisted through the leafless trees. A sad smile pulled at the hard corners of his mouth. "That's what I thought, too," he said at length, his hazel eyes reaching for hers. "But things changed." With an expressive lift of his broad shoulders, he leaned forward and prodded the horse into a slow gallop just as the path gave way to an open field bordering the stables.

Megan urged Mariah forward, and the quarter horse responded eagerly. The black mare raced through the snow with a quick burst of speed that closed the gap and brought her alongside the longer-strided Cody. "Race you," Megan called to Garrett with a laugh as Mariah sensed the thrill of a contest and spurted ahead of the big buckskin.

Megan heard the sound of Garrett's laughter as she leaned forward over Mariah's neck and the stout black mare sprinted toward the stables. The cold wind rushed at her face and caught in the auburn strands of her hair, but Megan didn't care. She felt younger, happier than she had in years. The race was exhilerating!

The sound of Cody's thundering hoofbeats warned Megan of Garrett's approach, but the tough-spirited Mariah wasn't easily beaten. The little mare dug in and managed to make it back to the stables a few seconds ahead of the gelding.

Garrett's eyes were dancing with laughter and admiration when he reined Cody to a halt and dismounted. "Well, ma'am," he drawled in an affected Western accent, "you done a right smart bit of ridin' back there."

Megan winked broadly and swung to the ground. "I think some of the credit should go to Mariah," she said fondly as she patted the mare's glistening rump. Mariah tossed her head menacingly into the air as if to give credence to Megan's words.

Garrett took the reins of both horses in one hand and grabbed Megan's shoulders with the other. They walked to the stables with their arms entwined and Megan smiled comfortably. Never had she been happier than these last few, fleeting hours with Garrett. Away from the pressures of the city and the office, she had rediscovered that special feeling they had shared three years ago. It was easy to think that she and Garrett were falling in love, all over again . . .

"I'll take care of these fellas," Sam Jordan announced. He had been repairing some of the equipment in the toolshed, but had come toward the stables when he heard all the noise. He was a grizzled man of about seventy-five. Though he walked with a slight limp and his skin was weathered, his bright blue eyes sparked with youthful mischief.

"Who won?" he asked with a devilish grin as he took the reins from Garrett. Mariah nuzzled the old man affectionately and Sam produced a carrot from his pocket for each of the horses, including Winthrop, a twenty-year-old roan who spent most of his days inside his stall.

"It was a victory for women's lib," Garrett replied as he removed the saddle from Cody's broad back.

"Was it, now?" Sam chuckled. He turned his attention to Megan. "I'm not surprised. That little lady—"he nodded in the direction of Mariah "—she's full of fire. Doesn't like to be beaten."

"None of us do," Megan responded with a merry laugh.

"And Cody." Sam shook his head, removed his hat and rubbed his fingers over his scalp. "He's got the speed, but he's just plain lazy—aren't you, boy?" Sam ran his palm fondly down the sleek tan coat of the horse in question. "It's all right. You'll beat her yet."

"Not likely," Garrett interjected with a playful frown.

"Maybe all he needs is a decent jockey," Sam suggested with a laugh.

"Good idea. Next time, you ride him."

"That I will," Sam mumbled, leading the horses into the stable. "That I will."

When Sam was out of earshot, Megan linked her hand through the bend in Garrett's elbow. "You're fond of him, aren't you?"

"Who, Sam?" Garrett's grin was slightly sheepish. "He and his wife, Molly, have been good to me for as long as I can remember." He pulled Megan toward the house. "Sam and Molly Jordan never change. Salt of the earth. The kind of people who would never let you down. People like that are hard to find."

That night, sitting with their backs propped against the couch, Megan and Garrett watched the dying embers of the fire. Garrett had pushed the couch forward, and Megan was able to lean her head against the soft leather cushions with her stockinged feet up against the warm flagstones of the hearth.

She balanced a chilled glass of Chablis in her hands, staring at the reflection of the red embers in the cut crystal and twirling the stem of her glass in her fingers. Not too long ago she had sat in this very room, nervously drinking wine and telling Garrett about the swindle. So much had happened since then, it seemed like ages ago. Now, huddled before the scarlet coals, even the silence was comfortable.

"I'm glad you came for me last night," Megan said, her eyes still studying the glass.

"I had to."

Her features drew into a pensive frown. "You didn't have to, but I have to admit that you were right."

"That's a first," he snorted. "About what?"

"You said that I needed to get away for a while." She paused as if she couldn't quite find the right words to convey all the feelings within her. "This time with you, Garrett, it's . . . well, it's been very special for me."

He set aside his glass and took her hand. "That's what I meant when I said that things have changed."

His thumb moved sensuously against her wrist. "I've lived here a long time, maybe too long."

Reluctantly he released her hand and drew his knees up to rest his chin against them. "A lot has happened to me under this roof." He frowned into the fire. "And when you left me—the first time, when Patrick was killed—it was difficult to stay here. I forced myself, and after a while I got used to the fact that you weren't coming back. Lana called me, we got together, and I decided that I needed to settle down. For good. I was bound and determined, dear lady, to get you out of my system once and for all."

"By substituting another woman?" Megan was incredulous.

"By any means possible." His eyes had narrowed with the painful memories. "Anyway, it didn't work, and maybe that was my problem. Maybe Lana knew how I felt. I don't know and I don't suppose it matters—not a whole hell of a lot." He ran his thumb along the edge of his jaw as he considered the succession of events that ended with the divorce. "The marriage was a mistake."

Megan swallowed with difficulty and her voice grew hoarse. "Are you trying to convince me that you didn't love her?"

"I didn't." When he noticed her surprise, Garrett added, "I tried to convince myself that I loved her; certainly I had feelings for her. Anyway, she told me that breaking off the engagement had been a mistake —mine, mind you—and that we should give it another shot. Since you made it pretty clear that you didn't want to see me again, I capitulated. Once thing led to another and we decided to get married."

"Just like that?"

His lips thinned angrily. "Sorry if I offended you. I don't remember my marriage to Lana as any big romance."

"It's just hard for me to understand."

"We all make mistakes, Megan. I shouldn't have to remind you of that."

The point hit home. Megan remained silent while Garrett kneeled before the fire and stoked the charred logs.

"I was stupid enough to think that a wife and family were what I wanted."

Megan felt something die within her. "But they weren't?"

"Are you kidding? The marriage was over almost before it began." He shook his head at his own folly. "I'll grant you that it wasn't all Lana's fault. We wanted different things in life. Lana wanted a career. I thought I wanted children. The two didn't mix, and I guess I wasn't very patient.

"I tried to understand when her work would take her to New York or Chicago. She was a free-lance journalist. She was an economics major in college and so most of her articles were on economics— from a woman's point of view. She became quite popular, what with the women's movement and all, and it didn't take her long to decide that she could support herself and shed the man who was hounding her for a family." He sat down beside Megan once again. "Seems that I'm attracted to the independent, career-oriented type, doesn't it?" He didn't wait for a response. He saw the shadows in her eyes. "So you can see why I thought about getting rid of the house."

"Not really," she muttered.

"When Lana and I were separated, it seemed to me that the only solid thing in my life was this house." He paused and looked up at the ceiling as if by staring at the weathered timbers he could make some sense out of his life.

Megan felt her throat constricting. Her voice was barely a whisper. "So what made you change your mind?"

"You."

The single word sent a shiver down her spine.

"When you walked back into my life, I thought that, despite the impending scandal, regardless of the past, we could work things out. I thought that if you just came back here and stayed with me, we could find what we gave up."

Megan tucked a wayward strand of hair behind her ear. "But you're considering moving."

He turned his darkened eyes upon her. "I was. The first night you were here, when you brought me the statements, didn't go as I had hoped. You left before we could really talk."

"You can't expect me to believe that you wanted to work things out between us," she said with a small laugh. "If I remember correctly, you were furious about the scam and the investigation. In fact, you threatened to sue me."

He couldn't deny the truth. He heaved a weary sigh and shook his head. "I said some things I shouldn't have."

"Does that mean there won't be a lawsuit?"

"What it means is simply that we, you and I, just can't help hurting each other."

"You mean that the lawsuit was an idle threat?"

"No. Just that you keep confusing what's happening to us professionally with what we feel on a personal level. One thing has nothing to do with the other."

She turned intelligent eyes on the rigid planes of his face. "So what are you telling me—what's all this leading up to?"

"Just that after your father's death, when we couldn't see each other for professional reasons, I decided that enough was enough and that I would find a way to get you out of my system. Once and for all. By selling the house, and purging any tangible evidence of what we had shared together, I thought I could forget you."

"But?" she prodded, her heart beating irregularly.

"But I made a costly mistake and went to your father's funeral. And there you were—with Ted Benson, no less."

"I wasn't *with* him."

"It looked like it from where I stood."

"He drove me home. Said he wanted to talk about Dad's will . . ."

"Did he?"

Megan smiled ruefully when she remembered the scene in Ted's car. "At the very least—"

His eyes drilled into hers. "What's that supposed to mean?"

Megan frowned pensively. "That Ted made a pass at me, but I was able to dodge it."

Every muscle in Garrett's face tensed and his hands clenched into tight fists of fury. "That miserable lowlife! It would serve the bastard right if I did decide to take this thing to court!"

Megan attempted to change the course of the conversation. "Relax, would you? I handled it." Megan's voice was calm, but her eyes glittered with pleased amusement. The last emotion she had expected Garrett to display was jealousy.

"You're very sophisticated and cool about a married man trying to seduce you, for God's sake!"

"Garrett, look. I'm thirty years old. I'm used to fending off unwanted attacks on my virtue." She laughed at the frustration on his face. "Forget it. It won't happen again."

"How can you be sure?"

"I know Ted Benson. He's too smart an attorney to blow it with me. Ted's partial to his life-style, and McKearn Investments is one of his most lucrative clients. I doubt that he'll jeopardize his yearly retainer for the sake of a good-night kiss."

"I'm sure he had more than a kiss in mind," Garrett growled.

"Doesn't matter. I'm only interested in one man."

The consternation on Garrett's face slowly dissipated and his eyes darkened seductively. "You know just what to say, don't you?"

"Only with you," she promised as she felt his lips brush against hers. "Only with you."

Sunday afternoon came much too quickly, and the relaxed atmosphere in Garrett's home began to melt with the snow. They had made love deep into the night, and the taste of passion was still on Megan's lips when she opened her eyes.

Once again, after a hearty breakfast, Garrett had taken her on a horseback ride. This one was much slower paced, and Megan had to fight Mariah to keep the spirited horse from bolting once she eyed the field where the race had taken place just the day before.

Garrett broiled steaks for dinner and served them on a platter laden with fresh parsley and buttered noodles. The meal was excellent, but conversation lagged as the time to return to the city drew near.

"I want you to come back, Megan," Garrett stated, once the table was cleared and Megan had mumbled something about having to get back to Denver.

"I'll think about it."

Garrett wasn't easily put off. He placed a comfortable arm around her shoulders and she leaned her head familiarly against his chest. "I'm not talking about a night, or a weekend, or even a temporary arrangement. I want you to move in permanently."

The words she had been waiting to hear for three years took her by surprise. Megan shifted away from him uneasily. He was offering what she wanted most in life, and yet she couldn't accept. "I'd like to," she whispered, "but I can't. Not yet."

"Why not?" The muscles in Garrett's back stiffened with suspicion.

"There's more to consider than just what I want to do. I have to think about the business—"

"To hell with the business."

"—and my mother."

"Isn't your aunt living with her?"

"For the time being, but I can't throw any more problems in her direction."

"Living with me wouldn't be a problem, and certainly not *hers!*"

Megan was tempted, sorely tempted. The life she had imagined was at her fingertips. All she had to do was say the word. Her smile was wistful, and unshed tears of love glistened in her round eyes.

"I just need a little time," she whispered, hoping that she wasn't throwing away her one chance at happiness. "There are so many things you and I have to work out."

"How much time, Megan?"

"I . . . I don't know."

He studied the honesty in her eyes. Strong fingers wrapped around her forearms, and his hazel eyes reached into hers. "As long as I know that you're not stalling and that you want to live with me . . ."

"Oh, Garrett, of course I do. You know that. More than anything—"

"Except the business."

"I just want to get the scam behind us."

" Because you don't trust me."

"Because I don't want to start off on the wrong foot."

"Like three years ago?"

"Exactly."

His dark brows blunted for a moment as he regarded her, but the fact that she returned his unwavering stare and managed a sad smile convinced him that she was being sincere.

"All right, Megan. We'll play it your way—for a little while."

Her teeth sank into her lower lip as Garrett pulled her into his strong embrace and his lips lingered against her hair. "I love you, you know," he murmured, "but I'm not a patient man."

Chapter Eleven

*M*egan had never gotten over Patrick's death. Not completely. And the guilt she silently bore hadn't lessened despite all of Garrett's arguments. She couldn't forget that it was she who had let Patrick down when he needed her most. Even now, as busy as her days were at the office, when she got home at night her thoughts would involuntarily shift to Garrett and the night three years ago when her brother was killed. The brief happiness she had shared with Garrett couldn't displace her sense of guilt.

Tonight was no different from any of the other nights. She sat alone in her apartment, huddled beneath a patchwork quilt while staring listlessly at the television. Though she tried to push thoughts of Garrett and Patrick aside, they continued to nag at her subconscious, disturbing her concentration.

With a pointed remark aimed at herself, Megan pressed the buttons on the remote control for the television, but each detective program or sitcom looked like the last and failed to capture her attention.

"You're a damned fool," she scolded. With a self-mocking smile, she clicked off the set, put down the remote control and picked up a magazine from the untidy stack on the coffee table.

It had been over a week since she had seen Garrett. He had called several times, but the conversations had been short and stilted, leaving Megan to second-guess herself and wonder if she had made the wrong decision. Maybe Garrett was right. Perhaps she should just ignore the problems at the business, the investigation, everything except her love for him. It was a pleasant thought and it brought tears of yearning to her eyes. If only things were so simple. In disgust, she tossed the magazine back onto the table.

What was she waiting for? An engraved invitation? She eyed the telephone and even went so far as to pick up the receiver before casting aside all thoughts of calling Garrett. It was ten o'clock at night and what could she say? I just wanted to hear your voice? I miss you? I love you?

She shook her head and set the receiver back in the cradle. The timing wasn't right. It might be weeks before the investigation would be complete, and she wanted to start her new relationship with Garrett on a positive note, with no doubts to cloud their future. . . .

After pouring herself a cup of tea, Megan leaned against the counter and stared out of the kitchen window into the night. *Patrick*. Why couldn't she forget about the tragic set of circumstances surrounding her brother's death? Frowning into her tea leaves, Megan sighed and swirled the hot, spicy liquid in her cup.

Patrick had been the apple of his father's eye. Even though by nature Patrick had been reckless and carefree, Jed McKearn had made no bones about the fact that he expected Patrick to settle down someday and take over the helm of McKearn Investments. Patrick considered it his birthright, but somewhat of a joke. An amused twinkle would lighten his clear green eyes whenever Jed would introduce the subject of running the company.

For his daughter, Jed had chosen the perfect mate, a single man who was a successful engineer. Bob Kendrick was also Patrick's best friend.

The sparks Jed had anticipated between Bob and Megan had never ignited. Megan and Bob Kendrick had remained only good friends, neither person interested in deepening the relationship. Bob was more interested in running around with Patrick than spending time with Megan, which was just as well. When Megan met Garrett, all of her time and thoughts were spent on him. She had little to spare for Bob . . . or Patrick.

Megan closed her eyes as the truth hit her with the force of an arctic gale. *Patrick had needed her, and she had abandoned him. The result was that he had died senselessly.* Her hands were trembling as she wrapped her fingers around the cup, as if for comforting warmth.

The trouble with her brother had started when Patrick had come to Jed and admitted that he was involved with a girl who was barely seventeen. The involvement included an unwanted pregnancy. The girl, Felicia Sterns, was due to have Patrick's baby in the early summer.

Anna McKearn had been crushed. Megan could still remember how her mother's face had washed of color and the pain that had darkened her eyes as she leaned heavily against her husband for support. But Jed had stoically accepted the news. Felicia's parents forced the issue, insisting that Patrick take responsibility for his unborn child and marry their daughter. Though Jed didn't approve of the hasty marriage, it was his hope that Patrick would finally settle down and become interested in working at McKearn Investment Company. As a new husband and father-to-be, Jed had reasoned, Patrick's reckless days were over.

It hadn't happened. According to Bob Kendrick, Patrick balked at the last minute. He didn't want to be strapped with a baby or a wife. He wasn't yet ready to shoulder that kind of responsibility—not for Felicia or anyone else.

Patrick had confided to Bob that he was tired of being pushed by Jed into a role he couldn't accept. To add insult to injury, Patrick had found out that Megan was seeing Garrett Reaves, a man Patrick had known through a mutual acquaintance, Lana Tremaine.

Patrick was livid when he confronted Megan with the condemning newspaper clipping, and when Megan ignored Patrick's warnings and ran off to meet her lover, Patrick started drinking and didn't stop. Then he set out to find Megan. Felicia was with him, and though Bob Kendrick tried to stop his friend, Patrick pushed Bob out of the way, climbed into the car with Felicia and roared off into the night.

The Jaguar slid off the road less than ten miles from Garrett's home and both Patrick and Felicia were killed instantly. Felicia's parents sued the estate of Patrick McKearn, and the scandal hit the papers with the force of a bolt of lightning. No one was left unscathed. Even Garrett's name was mentioned.

From that point on, Jedediah McKearn's health deteriorated and Anna McKearn became a shell of her former self. When Jed suffered his first heart attack, Megan took over the business on a temporary basis, but she had always hoped that Jed would resume his rightful place as the president of McKearn Investments. Now he was dead.

The sharp ring of the telephone startled Megan out of her unpleasant reverie. She jumped at the sound and put down her empty teacup as she reached for the phone.

"Hello?" Her voice sounded shaky. She clutched the ivory-colored receiver in a death grip.

"Glad I caught you at home." The warm sound of Garrett's voice forced a smile to her lips despite her morbid thoughts of the past. "How would you like to go to Rio?"

"Rio de Janeiro?" Megan asked, caught off guard.

"Do you know of any other?" he answered, the laugh in his deep-timbred voice infectious.

If only she could. "When?"

"Monday."

Megan closed her eyes as grim reality settled on her shoulders. "Garrett, I can't. Not now. I thought maybe you were talking about six months from now—"

"It can't wait," he interjected. Megan could hear the irritation in his voice. "I've got to look at a site for another plant. I thought it would be a chance for us to get away—together, alone—without worrying about the investigation."

"It sounds wonderful . . ."

"But?" he challenged. Megan could imagine the glint of anger in his eyes.

"I just can't get away. At least not for another month or so."

"Sorry. It's now or never." His voice was clipped, as if he were impatient to get off the phone.

Now or never. The words sounded so final. Desperation clutched at her throat and her knuckles whitened as she gripped the phone. "You know that I want to be with you," she whispered.

The only response was a ragged sigh.

"Garrett?"

"Forget it, Megan. And just for the record, I don't know anything about how you feel. Not one damned thing. Not anymore. Sometimes I think I'm dealing with a stranger." There was a short pause before he added, "Maybe it's better that way."

Without a word of goodbye, he hung up and

Megan was left with a haunting fear that she might not ever hear from him again.

Garrett had been out of the country for nearly two weeks, and though Megan's work at the office was more than enough to fill her hours, she felt incredibly alone. She had only heard from Garrett once, late at night, and the telephone conversation had been more than uncomfortable. The connection from Rio was bad, the conversation interrupted by frequent crackling noises, and the phone lines had seemed to hum with unspoken accusation.

The short, tense talk had left Megan aching for him. Had it only been a few weeks since those passion-filled nights and happy days at his home near Boulder? How, in such a short period of time, had things gone downhill so rapidly? And how much of it was her fault for not accepting Garrett's proposal to live with him? What more could she want?

Each day that passed without Garrett became more tedious than the last, and Megan was left with the uneasy feeling that something was wrong . . . terribly wrong.

Ted Benson stretched his long legs in front of him. He didn't seem particularly pleased with the news he had brought, but Megan was ecstatic.

"You have to realize that this is very preliminary," Ted warned, his watery blue eyes squinting as he lit a cigarette and waved the match in the air. Since the incident in his car on the day of Jed's funeral, the attorney had been less arrogant than usual and had kept his meetings with Megan on a strictly professional level. He sat slumped in one of the wing chairs near her desk and inhaled deeply on the cigarette before blowing a stream of pale blue smoke toward the ceiling.

"But it looks as if the SEC might not name Garrett in the suit." Megan's heart was beating triumphantly. Soon, Garrett would be proved innocent of any part in the scam.

"*If* there is a suit at all. You know, at this point, nothing's written in stone."

"But it looks good, right?" Megan slid her reading glasses up her nose and tapped her pencil on the desk. Why did she sense that Ted was warning her of something?

"It looks like Reaves won't be named—if *that's* what you consider good. You have to remember, Megan, McKearn Investments hasn't been cleared of any wrongdoing, at least not yet. And as for Reaves, well, anything can happen."

"What does that mean?" Megan's exhilaration slowly melted into dread. She let the pencil fall onto the desk and quietly clasped her hands together as she stared boldly into the attorney's cold eyes.

"Just because it *seems* the SEC might not go after Reaves, that doesn't mean it wòn't happen—especially if some new evidence is discovered linking Reaves to the scam. And then there's the question of criminality."

"Whether the swindle is a civil suit or a—"

"Felony." The word cut through the air like a knife and Megan paled slightly.

"George Samples may be up on criminal charges?"

"A very concrete possibility," Ted allowed, flicking the ashes of his cigarette into the tray. "Only the SEC knows what course of action it will recommend, and then the courts will decide what will happen. So," Ted said, pleased that he finally had all of Megan's attention, "you see that we're not out of the woods yet." As an afterthought he added, "And neither is Reaves." With a confident smile, Ted ground out his cigarette and slipped his arms through the sleeves of his imported raincoat.

"But it could be just a matter of time," Megan thought aloud, hoping she didn't sound as desperate as she suddenly felt.

Ted shrugged his shoulders in a dismissive gesture. "*Could* is relative, Megan. You might remember that. Too many people go around living their lives wondering what could have been instead of concentrating on the here and now." He grabbed his notes, stuffed them into his briefcase and headed for the door of her office. "I wouldn't go out celebrating tonight. You still have a tough row to hoe ahead of you."

"I'll remember that," Megan said, her eyes growing stern. "It's just that I'd like a little more good news for a change."

"Wouldn't we all," Ted muttered as he let himself out of the office.

Once the sober attorney had left, Megan picked up the phone and dialed the number of the airport. In a brief conversation she was told that Garrett's plane had been delayed for several hours because of a bomb scare at the airport earlier in the afternoon.

Regardless of Ted Benson's vague warnings or the

tense situation at the airport, Megan smiled to herself as she grabbed her purse and coat. With or without Ted's news concerning Garrett's innocence, Megan had finally come to the decision that, despite everything, she wanted to live with Garrett Reaves.

Ted Benson had been wrong about one thing, Megan decided as she walked to the elevator and into the waiting car: Tonight she was going to celebrate until dawn with the only man she had ever loved.

Stapleton International was a madhouse. Cars, buses and taxicabs jammed the parking lot. Angry horns blasted, and tires slid on the slick streets.

"Hey, lady, watch out!"

Megan heard the shout and an explicit oath as she pushed her way into the building. Not bothering to see if the warning were meant for her, she plowed her way through the confused mass of people milling in the terminal.

Between poor weather conditions and the bomb scare, the concourses were filled with anxious relatives, more anxious security guards and interested members of the press. Busy travelers, who had waited all afternoon to catch delayed flights, bustled through the terminal as they tried to claim baggage, connect with late incoming flights or just leave the airport. Shouts, angry grunts and muttered oaths were issued at random.

Pieces of conversations reached her ears, but she paid little attention to anything other than locating Garrett. She found the gate where Garrett's plane was to disembark and she waited nervously for the jet to land.

Oblivious to the commotion going on around her, she paced from one end of the windows to the other, alternately hiking her coat around her neck and checking her watch. A determined smile curved her lips and her eyes pierced the darkness as she waited impatiently for Garrett's return.

Her heart was hammering in her throat as she watched the 747 land and heard the roar of the engines fade.

Garrett was one of the first passengers to disembark. Though he strode rapidly up the ramp, he looked haggard and tired. A garment bag was slung haphazardly over one of his shoulders, and he carried his briefcase with his free hand. Dark circles shadowed his eyes, his mouth was compressed into a thin, hard line and his dark hair was rumpled.

He didn't notice her until an elderly gentleman who was blocking his path stepped aside. At that moment, Megan's eyes collided with his and for a heart-stopping instant a smile tugged at the corners of his mouth.

"You're a sight for sore eyes," he said, setting his bag and case on the ground.

It was all the encouragement she needed. Heedless of the crowd of onlookers, Megan threw herself into Garrett's arms. "I've missed you," she whispered hoarsely against his ear as his arms wrapped protectively around her. Tears of love filled her eyes. The arms holding her tightened and she heard him sigh wearily against the auburn strands of her hair.

"You don't know how long I've waited to hear you say that," he admitted, kissing her on the head.

Megan smiled through her tears, opened her eyes for just a moment and thought she recognized a face . . . a young, moustached man with dark eyes and a satisfied smirk who blended in with the crowd.

Garrett stiffened. "What's going on here?" he asked suddenly.

"What do you mean?"

"What's with all the photographers?" His hazel eyes scanned the crowd as he lifted his luggage in one hand, placed his other arm securely over Megan's waist and started toward the door.

Megan shrugged and tried to dismiss his unease. "There was a bomb scare earlier . . ."

"I know. I thought all the commotion had died down."

"The photographers are probably still hanging around, hoping for something to happen."

"Hmph." Garrett didn't seem convinced. "Let's get out of here." His voice had become wary and his restless gaze never left the ever-moving crowd. Suddenly his jaw hardened and his eyes narrowed.

"Garrett, what's wrong?" Megan asked, as he quickened his strides toward the doors leading out of the building. "What about your bags?"

"Got 'em." The cold air hit Megan in the face when the doors to the terminal opened. "Do you have your car here?"

"Yes—but wait a minute—"

"Where is it?" Garrett demanded.

"Over there, near the lamp . . ." Megan pointed a cold finger toward her car.

"Let's go." Garrett was already walking and Megan had to run to keep up with him. The darkness of the parking lot was lessened by the eerie light from the security lamps.

"Ms. McKearn!" a male voice shouted from somewhere near the doors of the terminal building. Megan stopped mid-stride.

"Ignore him, Meg," Garrett insisted, wrapping possessive fingers over her arm and nearly dragging her after him.

"Wait a minute. Who is it? And why are you acting so paranoid all of a sudden?"

"It's that damned reporter from KRCY news. If you want to stand around here and give him an impromptu interview, go right ahead. I'm not in the mood. Besides, I think one of those photographers back in the building snapped a picture of us together. In light of George Sample's accusations, I'm not all that crazy about the idea."

The cold night made Megan shiver. Garrett was the one who hadn't cared about the adverse publicity —or so he had claimed. Suddenly reporters made him uneasy. "Garrett, what's happening?" she asked.

"You tell me." Garrett's voice was harsh, his face an angry mask of determination. Dansen's rapid footsteps approached.

Garrett and Megan made it to the car just as Harold Dansen caught up with them. "Ms. McKearn, if you don't mind, I'd like to ask you a few questions."

"The lady does mind," Garrett interjected as Megan rifled through her purse looking for her keys. Her fingers were nearly numb from the cold.

"I'm asking her," Dansen remarked, and turned his dark eyes on Megan. "You've never given me that interview."

Megan managed a frozen smile. "My oversight."

"I would have thought McKearn Investments would want to tell its side of the story to the press. We've already had George Samples on the air."

"I can't do that. Not until the investigation is complete," Megan replied as she read the warning signs in Garrett's angry glare. "But once it is—"

"You'll call me, right?" Harold guessed with an I've-heard-it-all-before look that cut Megan to the core.

"Exactly," she stated with more authority than she felt.

"It's your funeral," Dansen returned.

Megan had opened the car door, but she stopped at the unprofessional remark. "Pardon me?"

"Nothing," Dansen replied with a condemning smirk. "Just remember, I gave you the chance to set the record straight."

"Which I will."

"Yeah, when the story's cold. Old news." He shrugged his shoulders indifferently. "Your choice." With his final words he turned on his heel and headed back to the terminal.

"Why do I have the feeling that I made the wrong decision?" Megan wondered aloud as Garrett slid into the driver's seat and turned on the ignition.

"Because that's the way he wants you to feel. The

guy knows how to manipulate people. I'll give him credit for that." Garrett maneuvered the car through the parking lot, paid the cashier and headed toward the heart of the city.

"You think it's an admirable quality?"

"What?"

"To manipulate people."

"Of course not. Just necessary sometimes." Megan was left with a cold feeling settling between her shoulder blades.

An uneasy silence settled over the black interior of the car. Tense minutes passed before Megan said, "Ted Benson was in to see me today."

All of the tired features on Garrett's face hardened. His eyes stayed on the road ahead of him. He shifted gears and the little car lurched forward. "What did he want?"

"To talk about the investigation."

"Is that all?" A hint of mockery edged his words. He turned the car onto the side street near Megan's town house.

"Yes. Damn it, Garrett, don't you trust anyone's motives?"

"Not when we're talking about Harold Dansen or that attorney of yours."

As Garrett parked the car, Megan turned to him and arched an elegant eyebrow. "This time you might be grateful to Ted."

"I doubt that."

"He seems to think you might be cleared of any charges." Megan smiled, but Garrett's eyes sparked in the dark interior of the car.

"He knows someone at the SEC?"

"A few people."

"And these sources have told him as much."

Megan was taken aback by Garrett's reaction. She had expected Garrett to be elated. Instead he seemed irritated. "To quote Ted, 'Nothing's written in stone.'"

"I'll bet." Garrett let out a long, ragged sigh and dropped his forehead onto the steering wheel. The frigid night seemed to seep through the windows.

"I think it's a positive sign," Megan whispered, her eyes fastened on the fatigued slump of Garrett's shoulders. She reached forward and, with hesitant fingers, quietly touched his temple.

"We're not out of the woods yet," he said quietly.

"It's a start, Garrett," she murmured, caressing his cheek. "And that's all we need."

He lifted his head, cocked it in her direction and studied the beautiful lines of her face. The searching look in his eyes begged her to explain herself.

"I've been doing some thinking since you've been gone," she stated, her gray eyes shining in the night.

"Go on."

"I was wrong about what would be best for us." Every muscle in his body froze. His eyes were stone cold, as if he were bracing himself for the worst. "I would love to come and live with you in Boulder," she whispered. "That is, if the offer is still open."

His hand softly touched her hair and his gaze wouldn't release her. "You're sure about this?" he asked with obvious reservation.

"More sure than I've been about anything in a long, long time." She placed her palms on either side of his face and slowly brushed her lips over his. "I love you, Garrett."

"Dear Lord, woman, why didn't you say so?" His arms captured her in an embrace as strong as it was gentle. Lips, suddenly swollen with desire, closed over hers and persuaded the kiss to deepen passionately. Her blood began to heat and pulse wildly in her veins.

Megan's eyes closed and she twined her arms around his neck. Her senses reeled with the thought that at last they were together . . . forever.

"Let's go inside," Garrett suggested, when he finally drew away from her. His hands were shaking as he rammed tense fingers through his hair in frustration.

They stood on the doorstep together, and Garrett leaned against the doorframe as Megan unlocked the door. He had expected several possible scenarios to develop once he returned from Rio, but never had he envisioned Megan's acceptance of his offer to live together. It didn't make a lot of sense, considering the tense phone calls they had shared.

Hating himself for his lingering doubts, he watched as Megan pushed the door open and turned her incredible eyes upon him. The smile on her face was irresistible, beckoning. He took one step toward her, then hesitated, giving her one last chance to change her mind.

As Megan stepped into the hallway, Garrett's hand reached out and captured her arm. She was in the house; he was still on the porch. Their eyes met. "You're sure about this?" he asked, solemnly studying the emotions on her face.

Her response was a gentle laugh that touched the darkest corner of his soul. "I've never been more sure of anything in my life."

Throwing aside his inner doubts, Garrett walked into the hallway, gathered Megan into his arms and kicked the door shut with his heel.

Chapter Twelve

*M*egan felt the mattress shift as Garrett rolled to the side of the bed. He didn't move for a minute, as if contemplating the sanity of waking so early, and then he stood and pulled on his pants. The belt buckle jingled slightly, breaking the stillness of the early-morning hours.

"What're you doing?" Megan mumbled into the pillow, then turned to face him. The room was still dark, and a glance at the luminous face of the clock confirmed what she had guessed: It was barely dawn.

"Sad as it is," Garrett replied with honest regret heavy in his voice, "I've got to shower and change at my apartment before I go to the office." Garrett reached for his shirt, which had been slung over the high back of a chair near the vanity.

"Now?"

He chuckled softly. "Now."

She could barely make out his figure in the darkness—a black silhouette of a lean, well-muscled man against the soft illumination of the streetlamps filtering through the sheer curtains. "I'll get you breakfast . . ."

"Don't bother. I'll get something at work." He leaned over the bed and smoothed back her hair before placing a warm kiss against her forehead. "Go back to sleep."

Disregarding his suggestion, she pulled herself into a sitting position, held the satin comforter over her breasts and watched with obvious pleasure as he slipped into his dress shirt, fumbled with the buttons and carefully straightened his cuffs.

"Goodbye, Megan," he whispered, and the sound of his steps on the stairs echoed hollowly in Megan's mind. The bed seemed suddenly empty and cold.

I've got to get up anyway, she decided as she rolled to her side and grabbed the robe lying on the foot of the bed. When she got to the landing, she was cinching the tie around her waist.

Garrett was in the foyer. A small table lamp gave a warm illumination to the hallway. He had already retrieved his garment bag and coat, and he looked up at the sound of her footsteps on the stairs.

"I'll call you later," he promised.

Megan stood three steps above him, watching as Garrett shrugged into his raincoat. She fingered the belt of her robe, then, yawning, pushed her tousled hair out of her eyes.

"You could stay longer . . ." she invited, wondering at her sudden need of him. She didn't want to let go of the few precious hours they had shared. The love, the passion, the honesty of the night—she couldn't release them. Not yet.

Garrett shook his head but smiled broadly. His hand was poised over the doorknob, and he hesitated for a moment. "Don't tempt me," he cautioned, his lips compressed pensively. "I just might take you up on it."

"Then why not?" Megan observed him through the silky curve of black lashes still heavy from recent slumber.

"Something you'll understand very well, I think. It's called responsibility."

"Business before pleasure?"

"In this case, I think we've already had pleasure before business," he pointed out. "I'll see you later." Garrett opened the door and a cold rush of morning air blew into the house. "Here." He picked up the rolled newspaper from the doorstep and tossed it to Megan. Then he was gone.

The door shut with a thud and Megan was left with only the cold newspaper in her hands and an emptiness deep within her soul. She shuddered from the cold air and the feeling of loneliness stealing over her. "Dear Lord, Megan," she chided, mounting the stairs, "you've lived without him for over three years. Certainly a few hours won't make a difference."

After scanning the newspaper and placing it on a small table, she went into the bathroom to shower and change for work.

Before she left for the office, Megan made herself a light breakfast and decided to call to her mother. It had been several days since she had seen Anna, and

Megan wanted to make sure that her mother's spirits hadn't flagged.

It wasn't quite seven. Although it was early, Aunt Jessica was usually up and about before dawn. Jessica complained of insomnia, but Megan suspected that her aunt was just one of those people who thrived on only a few hours of sleep.

"Good morning," Megan called into the phone, once Jessica had answered.

"Megan. I was wondering when we would hear from you."

"I called yesterday. No answer."

"Must've been when we were out shopping." Jessica chuckled.

"Did Mom go with you?" Megan asked, concern sharpening her voice.

Aunt Jessica understood. "Did she ever. Nearly bought out the stores." And then, on a more somber note, "She's doing okay, considering."

"I thought I'd drop by after work."

"Wonderful!" Aunt Jessica was once again her lively self. "It's been nearly a week since you've shown your face around here."

"You're right," Megan admitted, feeling a twinge of guilt.

"Don't worry about it. Anna and I have kept ourselves busy," Jessica assured her. Megan believed it. Aunt Jessica never seemed to run out of energy.

"Then I won't be interrupting your plans if I come over?"

"Never, child. Oh, by the way, I'm trying to talk your mother into taking a trip to the islands. You know, either before or after Christmas. I think she'd enjoy the sunshine for a change. Do her a world of good," Jessica predicted with authority.

"I'm sure it would," Megan agreed. Her mother had always wanted to visit Hawaii, but Jed's attention to his business had always interfered with the trip. And then, when he did retire, his health had declined to the point that Anna wasn't interested in anything other than caring for her ailing husband.

"Then you'll give her that extra nudge?" Jessica asked.

Megan laughed. "Count on it. Listen, I've got to get ready for work. See you two later."

It was nearly eight when she finally got into her car and braved the inclement weather conditions. The snow had fallen throughout the night, but for the most part, traffic flowed smoothly. Megan wheeled the little car into the parking lot of the Jefferson Tower just a little later than usual.

Nothing seemed out of the ordinary until she stepped out of the elevator on the eighth floor and realized that the reporters were back. A hodgepodge of anxious journalists crowded around the door to the investment company, and Megan guessed that there were more media people pacing uncomfortably just inside the glass doors. And they were waiting for her.

Megan forced a polite smile on her face as she pulled off her gloves and observed the reporters. A few had noticed her arrival and were heading her way. Fortunately, there weren't as many journalists today as there had been on the day George Sample's story hit the papers. However, there were enough inquisitive faces, note pads and photographers to test Megan's resolve. She strode purposefully toward the small crowd. Interested eyes turned in her direction.

"Here she is," someone whispered to his peers.

"Ms. McKearn," a young, well-dressed woman with intelligent blue eyes accosted her. "Is it true that you're seeing Garrett Reaves?"

"Pardon me?" Megan was taken aback. Her patient smile faltered slightly.

The blond smiled. "Rumor has it that you're romantically involved with Mr. Reaves. True?"

Megan managed to pull her crumpled poise into place and forced a thin, professional smile for the woman and the rest of the members of the press. "Mr. Reaves and I are friends." A noncommittal lift of her shoulders accompanied the statement, as if anything else that might be implied by the question were totally out of line.

"Despite the investment swindle?" the young woman persevered, undaunted by Megan's nonchalance. The blond was writing furiously in a notebook.

Megan eased her way to the door of the investment firm. "I've known Garrett Reaves for over three years."

"Then you knew him when he was married to Lana Tremaine," Harold Dansen stated, his black eyes focusing on Megan.

Though she felt herself withering inside, Megan met the reporter's suspicious gaze squarely. A thousand questions raced through her mind. *Why were the reporters here this morning? What had happened? And why did the mention of Garrett's ex-wife cause a feeling of cold dread to chill her from the inside out?*

"I knew him then," Megan responded without batting an eye. Though her palms were sweating, she maintained the image of a confident executive. "If you'll excuse me, I have work to do."

"Were you lovers?" the blond asked, and though Megan's complexion paled slightly, she moved her eyes away from the presumptuous young woman.

"One more question, Ms. McKearn," Dansen persisted, fingering the thick strands of his moustache. "Did you know that Lana Tremaine was George Samples's accomplice?"

"What?" Megan whispered before she recovered herself. The accusation hit her like a bolt of lightning and she had to force herself to face the anxious eyes of the press.

"I asked if you knew that Lana Tremaine, Garrett Reaves's ex-wife, was involved in Samples's swindle?"

Megan's heart was beating so rapidly she was sure everyone could hear it. All eyes were on her. Lana Tremaine! A part of the investment scam! Maybe it was a mistake. She hadn't read about it in the paper this morning. She heard herself speaking while crazy thoughts, filled with suspicions and doubts, flitted through her mind.

"As you know, Mr. Dansen, I'm not at liberty to discuss Mr. Samples or the alleged scam. Excuse me." Not waiting for any further questions to be thrust in her direction, Megan pushed her way past the reporters. When she got into the office she told the receptionist that she wouldn't meet with any newspaper people until late in the afternoon.

Megan felt strangled, and when she read a later edition of the paper alleging that Lana Tremaine had, in fact, been a part of the scam, her stomach knotted so painfully that she had to sit down.

Don't go off the deep end, she warned herself. Maybe this is all a mistake. And, even if it's not, it doesn't mean that Garrett's involved.

Forcing a calm facade over her elegant features, Megan asked Jenny for a cup of coffee and instructed the receptionist to call Henry Silvas and Ted Benson immediately.

When she got each of the men on the phone, she arranged for them to meet with her in her office.

The coffee did little to calm her nerves, and she was pacing back and forth in front of her desk when Jenny buzzed the intercom to announce that Henry Silvas had arrived.

"Please, send him in," Megan suggested, her voice strained.

Henry entered the office, rubbing his thinning hair frantically.

"Good morning," Megan said.

"Morning."

Megan stopped her pacing long enough to level a searching glance at the accountant. "Can you tell me what the devil is going on?" she asked. "The press have been camping out near the elevators for hours."

"Just heard about it myself—from Ted Benson.

He should be here soon. He said he tried to call you but couldn't get through."

"I know. I got through to his secretary a few minutes ago." Megan sighed and dropped into her chair. "He must have called me at the apartment while I was talking to Aunt Jessica."

"Doesn't matter. Here's the story." Henry fumbled in the inside pocket of his suit jacket, withdrew a cigar and began puffing furiously on the imported blend of tobaccos. "It seems that the SEC has found George's accomplice." Henry's dark eyes, magnified by his wire-rimmed glasses, were troubled.

Megan's fingers tapped restlessly on the edge of her desk as she waited for him to continue.

"Ever heard of Derrick Van Weiss?"

Megan shook her head and rubbed her temples. The name was unfamiliar.

"Didn't think so. He's only written a couple of columns for the *Denver Financial Times*. A freelancer. Works out of New York."

"No, never heard of him."

"He's not very well-known, but once in a while a few of the papers run his stuff."

"I still don't understand—"

"Van Weiss was only *one* of Samples's partners."

"So who else was involved?" Dread took a stranglehold on her heart. She knew the answer.

"Lana Tremaine Reaves."

Megan's face lost all its color. "How?" she whispered. The newspaper article had been sketchy, obviously added after the first edition had been printed.

Henry sighed and set his cigar in the ashtray. "It's not as complicated as it sounds, but it appears that Van Weiss is the brains behind the operation. It might involve more than one paper. Anyway, Van Weiss and Lana Reaves know each other. One of them—probably Lana because she's from here and knew George Samples in the beginning—approached Samples with the idea. He took to it—"

The door to the office whispered open and Ted Benson strode into the room. "That George did," Ted agreed with a shake of his head. "Created a damned mess." Ted slid into a chair near Henry and his stony blue eyes impaled Megan. "The hell of it is that I think the SEC will find that others are involved."

Megan felt as if the bottom had dropped out of her world. Without saying it aloud, Ted Benson was implying that suspicion had once again reverted to Garrett. Her stomach lurched and she had to swallow against the dryness in her throat. "So we're not out of the woods yet," she said, inadvertently quoting Garrett.

"Not by a long shot," Ted said with a frown. He tugged at his tie in a gesture of self-importance. "And, I'm afraid the press will demand that you make some sort of statement. Don't do it. Not yet. I'll handle that part. It's going to look bad for McKearn Investments, no doubt about it. Not only did the broker work here, but several accounts were involved, including that of Garrett Reaves—Lana Tremaine's husband."

"Ex-husband," Megan pointed out.

"Could get sticky," Henry thought aloud.

"It already has," Megan said with a weary sigh. No wonder the reporters were questioning her relationship with Garrett. Her stomach began to knot painfully, and she nervously ran her fingers through her neatly coiled hair.

"You'll have to be careful, Megan," Ted warned. "Anything you say or do will be under scrutiny from the press."

"I know."

"Especially concerning Garrett Reaves."

"That's right," Henry agreed, puffing thoughtfully on his cigar. "Your mother told me you were seeing him. You'll have to be discreet."

"Or end the relationship," Ted offered. "At least temporarily. No reason to add fuel to the fire."

"You think Garrett's involved, don't you?" Megan asked, eyeing the two men boldly but already knowing the answer. A sinking feeling of betrayal settled on her slim shoulders.

"It's conceivable that Reaves worked with his ex-wife. At least it looks that way to me," Henry answered honestly, and he noticed the pain in Megan's eyes. "I'm sorry, Meg, but I call 'em as I see 'em."

"Agreed," Benson interrupted. "Reaves apparently used information from his ex-wife to make money in the market, via George Samples."

"So now you've decided he's guilty." Megan's voice was low and sounded tired. "Just yesterday you were suggesting that the SEC might drop the investigation—as far as Garrett Reaves was concerned."

"A man is innocent until proven guilty," Ted

assured her, "but you can't refute the evidence stacking up against Reaves. As for what I thought yesterday, it's of no consequence. It happened *before* the SEC collared Van Weiss and linked him to Lana Reaves."

"That still doesn't mean—"

"Look, Megan," Henry interrupted. "I told you in the beginning that Reaves might be involved. His account was one of the nine that made money off of George's inside information." The accountant shifted uneasily in his chair. The last thing he wanted to do was make it more difficult for Megan, but he had no choice. He dealt in dollars and cents and the truth.

"True, but—"

"And, he did sell short on Reaves Chemical stock."

"After filing the necessary papers."

Ted Benson frowned. "Other people made money on that trade—George Samples's special clients."

"Probably because George advised them to." Megan couldn't control her urge to defend Garrett.

"Anyway around it, Megan," Henry stated, "Mc-Kearn Investments is on the hook. No matter what actually happened, it looks as if George interpreted the selling short as a signal from Reaves and he passed the information along. In return, Reaves became one of George's special clients and was awarded favors."

"In the form of big profits on trades made based on the inside information gained from Lana Tremaine Reaves and Derrick Van Weiss," Megan surmised.

"Exactly." Ted Benson lit a cigarette and pondered Megan's quiet composure. She was in a state of shock, that much was obvious, but there was still a defiant lift to her chin and a promise of steel-hard determination in her soft gray eyes. The woman had more grit than Ted ever would have guessed. "That's why you've got to be careful. Until the investigation is complete, anything you do will be under scrutiny by the SEC as well as the press."

Courageously, Megan met the concerned eyes of the two men sitting opposite her. She knew in her heart that what they were suggesting was for the good of the firm—and herself as well—and yet she couldn't believe that Garrett was caught in the intricate web of intrigue and scandal Derrick Van Weiss, Lana Tremaine and George Samples had woven.

She turned her attention to the attorney. "Speaking strictly as legal counsel for McKearn Investments, what course of action would you advise?"

"Low profile for you," Ted answered as he ground his cigarette into the ashtray. "As for the investment firm, it's business as usual. Investor confidence is imperative."

Henry Silvas pursed his lips together, clasped his hands, and nodded his head in mute agreement.

"But you don't think I should assure the press that we're operating as if nothing has happened?"

Ted shook his head. "I'll take care of it. You can issue a statement in a couple of days, once all the furor has died down. Right now your main concern is angry clients who may read the paper and misunderstand the facts."

"And if it doesn't die down—the furor, that is?" Megan wondered aloud.

"We'll cross that bridge when we come to it." Ted cocked his wrist, checked his watch and grabbed his briefcase. "I'll handle the press for now—but remember, they're gunning for you."

"Don't I know it," Megan muttered, remembering the look of cruel satisfaction in Harold Dansen's eyes this morning. What had he said last night at the airport? Something about its being her funeral? Well, he hadn't exaggerated. At least not much.

Henry Silvas and Ted Benson left the room, and after a few moments of hesitation, Megan lifted the receiver of the phone and dialed the offices of Reaves Chemical.

"I'm sorry," Megan was informed politely when she had asked to speak to Garrett, "Mr. Reaves hasn't come in this morning and I doubt that he'll be in all day."

"But I was under the impression that I could reach him there," Megan replied, her heart missing a beat.

"Not today. Mr. Reaves has been out of the country for a couple of weeks, you know. If you'd like to leave your name and number, I'll have him return the call."

"No, thank you," Megan whispered, her eyes blurring as she replaced the phone. The secretary acted as if she hadn't expected to see Garrett. Had he lied to Megan this morning? It just didn't seem possible. After a night of honest confessions of love, why would he lie? Megan shook her head as if to clear out the cobwebs of confusion. Nothing made any sense.

After a moment's hesitation, she called Garrett's apartment in the city. No answer.

Without realizing the desperation of her actions, she grabbed the phone again and dialed the number of Garrett's home near Boulder. Perhaps he had changed his mind and decided to go back to his home. Megan's teeth sank into her lower lip as she counted the rings.

"Pick it up," she whispered. "For God's sake, Garrett, be there."

After ten rings, she replaced the receiver. She walked slowly to the window and stared out sightlessly, unaware of the snowflakes falling from a leaden sky or of the scattered pedestrians milling on the sidewalks far below her. She leaned her forehead against the cool glass and wondered, if only fleetingly, if Garrett had ever stopped loving Lana Tremaine.

Once before he had used Megan as an idle flirtation. Could he be doing it again? But why? One part of Megan, fiercely loyal to the man she loved, screamed that even the thought of Garrett's caring for his ex-wife was preposterous.

Hadn't Megan seen the look of love in his eyes last night when he held her in his arms and made slow, wonderful love to her? *He did it before. Remember the night of Patrick's death?*

Hadn't Garrett himself stated that Lana meant nothing to him, that the marriage was the result of Megan's rejection? *But that could have been a lie as well—a cover-up of the truth to avoid arousing Megan's suspicions.*

Then why had Garrett bothered to rekindle their

affair after three long years? *Because he needed her protection. He was banking on her vulnerability to him, and he had used it as a weapon against her.*

A silent tear slid down her face. Whether she wanted to or not, Megan was forced to consider the facts. The facts that Ted Benson, Henry Silvas, the Securities and Exchange Commission and the rest of the world would use to condemn Garrett Reaves.

Face it, Megan, the rational side of her nature admonished, *Garrett used you . . . again.*

Somehow, despite what seemed overwhelming odds, Megan got through the rest of the day. The phone hadn't stopped ringing, but Megan's secretary had fielded the calls from the press.

The one telephone call she had hoped to receive hadn't come through, and each time Megan had phoned Garrett's apartment or home, no one had answered.

She had tried to keep her mind away from thoughts of Garrett. At work it had been difficult, but dinner at her mother's house had helped a little. Even though Megan's spirits were depressed, seeing that her mother was adjusting to widowhood was comforting.

"I've just about convinced her," Aunt Jessica was teasing while she served thick wedges of deep-dish apple pie. The three women were sitting around the massive dining room table sipping coffee.

"Convinced me of what?" Anna asked.

"Why, of coming to Hawaii with me, of course." Jessica smiled slyly in Megan's direction. "What do you think?"

"A good idea," Megan stated, hoping she sounded more enthusiastic than she felt. "Perfect time of the year."

"I don't know if I can get used to Christmas lights on palm trees . . ."

"Oh, go on," Jessica laughed, tossing her shiny blond hair. "For your information, they ship fir trees to Hawaii, just like any other state. Besides, the sun will do you good."

"Humph. To listen to her, you'd think I needed a keeper," Anna said to her daughter, and all three women laughed.

Later, when Jessica was fussing over the dishes, Anna McKearn pulled her daughter aside. "What's going on, Megan?" she inquired, looking past the pretense of calm in Megan's eyes. "Trouble at the company?"

Megan lifted her shoulders and put on her coat. "A little."

"Or a lot?"

"Really, Mom, it's not that serious."

"Isn't it?" Anna patted her daughter's arm. "You're a lot like your father, you know. And I could read him like a book. This swindle business has got you down, hasn't it?"

Megan smiled wanly. "I'd be a liar if I didn't admit that I'll be glad when it's over."

"Amen," Anna breathed before kissing Megan on the cheek. Anna paused for a minute, and her expression became more sober. "I see that Garrett Reaves's name has come up."

Megan nodded, and Anna caught the small wince of rejection on her daughter's face.

"Are you seeing him again? He was with you at the hospital—"

"I'm not exactly sure . . . just what Garrett's feelings are right now. We're both busy."

"Of course you are." At that moment Aunt Jessica marched down the hall.

"Leaving, Meg?"

Megan nodded. "I'm a working woman, you know."

Jessica waved off her niece's excuses. "Next time don't make yourself so scarce."

"I won't."

After saying a hasty goodbye, Megan walked through the snow to her car and drove to her apartment—to face the long, cold night alone.

Chapter Thirteen

*W*hat to do?

Megan paced the living room floor of her apartment like a caged animal. Her phone calls trying to locate Garrett had been fruitless, and at this point, mindful of Ted Benson's and Henry Silvas's warnings against talking to Garrett again, Megan decided she would stop her attempts at tracking him down. Garrett knew where she was, and he had to know that she was waiting to hear from him.

After all, it was *he* who had promised to call. Last night, while lying in the security of Garrett's strong arms, Megan had put her heart on the line. Garrett had apparently decided to walk all over it.

Anger and fear colored her thoughts. Where was Garrett? What was he doing? With whom? Though her love for him was as strong as it ever had been, the questions rattling in her head made her faith waver. There had been too many lies in her relationship with him to trust him blindly.

The evening edition of the paper was lying on the coffee table. Almost as a reminder to Megan of how foolish she had been to trust Garrett, the headlines, bold and black, stated: *LANA REAVES SOUGHT IN SEC INVESTIGATION*.

The article outlined the basic story, but as an added aside, it noted that Lana Reaves's ex-husband, Garrett Reaves, had an account with McKearn Investments and that he was romantically linked with the president of the investment firm, Megan McKearn. Next to the lengthy article was a slightly blurred photo of Garrett and Megan embracing in the crowded concourse of Stapleton International Airport, only last night.

Megan groaned when she glanced at the photograph one last time. Her small fists clenched and she stamped one foot in frustration. "You're a fool," she chastised herself with a grimace. After all the agony in the past, how could she have let herself fall into the very same trap?

Because I love him, she thought painfully, and realized that she would never stop caring for Garrett. No matter how dirty the scandal became, despite all the malicious gossip and snide innuendos, she still loved him. Just as desperately as she had the first night she had been with him, three years ago. But though she would probably always love him, she couldn't allow herself to be entangled with him. Not now. Not ever. It was painfully clear that whatever blissful moments she had shared with Garrett were the last. She tried to convince herself that it was over—there was just no other way out of this mess.

Damning herself for her weakness, she turned on the television and sank onto the couch. The last half hour of the prime-time drama did nothing to catch her attention, and she shifted uneasily on the comfortable cushions while thumbing disinterestedly through a financial magazine.

When the phone rang, she started. Telling herself that it was probably just another reporter, Megan risked answering and silently prayed that it would be Garrett's voice on the other end of the line. Not only did she need to hear from him, but she had to tell him that she couldn't see him again. Not that he cared . . .

"Hello?"

Disappointment clouded Megan's features, and the small headache at her temple began to throb mercilessly. "Megan. Didn't wake you, did I?" Ted Benson's voice had an unsettling effect on Megan, and exasperation weighed heavily upon her.

"No—I'm still up." She managed to hold her voice steady while her foot tapped restlessly.

"Good. I thought I'd keep you abreast of the latest."

"I saw it in the evening papers." Once again Megan eyed the slanted article.

"It's not as bad as it looks."

Megan sighed. "Hard to believe, Ted, because it looks bad—damned bad."

The attorney's voice was firm. "Look, Lana Reaves has been found. She was in New York. The legal grapevine has it that Ron Thurston has agreed to defend her, should she be prosecuted."

"Oh, my God," Megan whispered, a chill as cold as the wintry night piercing her heart. "But he's a local attorney . . ."

"I know. Works for her husband. I suppose that's why Thurston's taking the case."

"But they're divorced," Megan protested weakly. Even to her it sounded like a frail defense.

"Megan, look, you'd better face facts. Lana Tremaine and Garrett Reaves were married. She's in trouble. So is he. Looks as if they're in this mess together." His voice had become softer, more consoling. "I know you don't like the sound of it, but I think Reaves used you to protect his ex-wife."

No! her heart screamed. Megan's head dropped into her hands. She twisted an auburn strand of hair nervously in her fingers and tried to remain calm. "Why are you telling me all of this, Ted?" she asked, feeling suddenly defeated.

"Because you've got to pull yourself together. If you thought today was tough, wait until tomorrow. The press will be standing at your doorstep."

"Ready to eat me alive?"

"Close enough."

"Dear God," she whispered.

"What ever happens, Megan, just stay cool. The reputation of McKearn Investments is on the line. Now that Jed's gone, you're it; the man in charge, so to speak. Everyone will be watching you—the press, the members of the board, the investors, the works. You're in the spotlight, whether you want to be or not. I'll help you any way I can, but in the end it's up to you to present the professional, full-of-integrity attitude that will convince the public that McKearn Investments is just as solid today as it was when Jed was running the corporation." He paused for a moment and then added, "You can do it, Megan, if anyone can."

"Thanks for the vote of confidence," she murmured before saying goodbye and hanging up.

Great! Things seemed to be going from bad to worse.

She went into the kitchen, made herself a pot of cinnamon tea and returned to the couch, settling in the corner and placing the steaming cup on the overstuffed arm. Memories of Garrett wouldn't leave her weary mind alone.

As she stirred the amber tea, images invaded and tormented her mind: sipping wine before the quiet flames of a dying fire; riding horseback through snow-laden pine trees. "Oh, Garrett," she moaned to herself. "Why couldn't it be easy for us?"

On the television, the eleven o'clock news was just going on. The local anchorwoman, a petite redhead with a winning smile, was sober tonight as she gave a quick rundown of the featured stories.

The first story made Megan's pulse jump. She nearly spilled the hot tea, and her eyes never wavered from the small television set. The petite redhead was talking rapidly.

"Garrett Reaves, local businessman and president of Reaves Chemical, stood by his ex-wife's side while she was interviewed by reporters concerning her involvement in the alleged investment scam that broke at the *Denver Financial Times* and McKearn Investments last month.

"Mrs. Reaves's involvement in the scam was undisclosed until late this afternoon, when she made a brief statement to the press."

The television screen switched from the anchorwoman to what was obviously a prerecorded tape. The scene was Stapleton International, and the man and woman dominating the screen were Mr. and Mrs. Garrett Reaves. Photographers and journalists crowded the couple, and the noise in the busy airport interfered slightly with the audio.

Megan felt her throat constrict as she saw the weariness of Garrett's features. He was holding onto Lana's elbow possessively as they shoved their way through the throng of reporters and interested travelers.

"Mr. Reaves," a reporter called, and Megan recognized the voice of Harold Dansen. She felt herself shrivel inside. Dansen, whose face now appeared on the screen, asked, "Could you or Mrs. Reaves comment on her involvement in the scam?"

"No comment," Garrett stated, looking squarely into the camera and attempting to break through the barrier of reporters blocking his path.

"Just a minute." Lana Reaves, a slender woman with a thick mane of glossy blond hair, placed a restraining hand on Garrett's coat sleeve. It was an intimate gesture, and it ripped Megan to the bone. The noise from the crowd seemed to hush as Lana boldly stared into the camera.

Her eyes were an intriguing shade of blue accented by thick brown lashes. Lana Tremaine Reaves was one of the most beautiful women Megan had ever seen. No wonder Garrett, or any man for that matter, couldn't resist her. Megan nearly burned her fingers by clenching the cup of tea so tightly.

"I have nothing to say at the moment," Lana stated calmly, her eyes looking steadily into the camera, "other than that I've made a full statement to the SEC. Any other questions can be answered by my attorney." With an arrogant toss of her head, she once again began moving, and Garrett was at her side, helping her out of the building and into a waiting car. The camera followed Garrett's movements until the car had been driven out of sight.

Megan sunk into the cushions. She felt drained and hoped that the story was complete. It wasn't. Before the feature was finished, a snapshot of Megan was flashed onto the screen while the anchorwoman gave a brief history of Megan's career, along with her alleged involvement with Garrett Reaves.

Also included in the story was a photograph of her father, and a mention of Patrick's tragic death.

"Not again," Megan murmured, witnessing with horror as personal shots of Jed and Patrick were flashed onto the screen.

Megan was shaking with indignation by the time the story was finished and the news had turned to the political scene.

Megan snapped off the set. She felt dead inside. Ted and Henry had been right. Garrett had used her, and she had been fool enough to let him. With a sigh, she turned out the lights and went upstairs.

It looked as if the cards were stacked against her, but Megan was determined to pull herself together and face whatever the press had in store for her tomorrow. No matter how shattered she felt inside, she would manage to show a strong image to the press, the investment clients, the members of the board and, most especially, to Garrett Reaves. Tears pooled in her eyes, but she forced them back. There was no room in her life for tears over a mismanaged love affair.

As she pulled on her nightgown and surveyed the bed in which she and Garrett had made love only the night before, a small cry broke from her lips. "Why must I love you?" she wondered aloud before sliding into the bed and holding on to her pillow as if for dear life.

A strange, loud noise throbbed in Megan's ears. She awoke with her heart in her throat. Her dream had been vivid and painful. Images of Patrick's car, a twisted red mass of metal against the stark white snow, had been dispersed and replaced by the cold, angry lines of Garrett's face.

The incessant pounding, which had brought her so rudely out of slumber, resumed, and Megan's tired mind suddenly registered. Someone was at the door, though it was four in the morning.

She was down the stairs in a flash, throwing her robe over her shoulders and slipping her arms through the sleeves as she raced to the window and flipped the light switch to illuminate the porch. She peeked through the window. There, standing on her step, his face just as angry as it had been in her dreams, was Garrett. Her heart turned over at the sight of him.

Opening the door just a crack, she let her gray eyes clash with his. He looked as if he hadn't slept since she had last seen him. He probably hadn't. The tiny lines near the corners of his eyes had deepened, and the set of his jaw showed that he was furious. The cold, damp morning air seeped through the small space between the door and the wall.

"Are you going to let me in?" he asked.

Megan was tempted, but reason tempered her response. "I don't think so."

He placed his hand against the door and rested his forehead wearily against his arm. "Why not?"

"Things have changed since last night."

"You're telling me," he admitted. "I think we need to talk."

"And I think it might be too late for it." Her voice shook, and her eyes, which she hoped would seem determined, were a misty gray and decidedly vulnerable.

His fist balled and pounded against the door. Megan felt the reverberations through the cold oak panels. "Damn it, woman, it's freezing out here and my patience is gone. Let me in and let's straighten this mess out."

Her fingers tightened over the doorknob. If she would just unhook the chain, he would be with her. Inside. Warm. Away from the rest of the world. She could pretend that what had happened yesterday was just a bad dream. . . . But it wasn't. She shook her head, and the blue light from the porch lamp caught in the coppery tangles of her hair. "We've been trying for weeks and weeks, and it seems like the more we try, the worse it gets."

"Maybe that's because we didn't have all the facts," he said wearily. "I'm too damned tired for games tonight, Megan. I think you should have the decency to listen to my side of the story. No doubt you've heard everyone else's."

Megan hesitated only slightly before releasing the chain. Silently the door swung inward and Megan stepped out of Garrett's path, mutely inviting him into her home.

Garrett strode into the foyer and clasped both hands over his head, stretching his tired back muscles. Tossing his down jacket over an oak hook on the hall tree, he turned to face Megan just as she closed the door.

They were alone.

Together.

It should have been enough, but the aloneness and the togetherness didn't begin to bridge the black, gaping abyss of misunderstanding that separated them.

"It's four in the morning," Megan admonished with a shake of her head.

"And I'm beat."

"You look it," Megan allowed. A dark shadow of beard covered the lower half of his face, and the spark that usually lighted his hazel eyes was missing. The corners of his mouth were hard and turned down, and deep marks furrowed his brow. His black hair was windblown, and he was wearing the same corduroy slacks and dress shirt he had been wearing when he left her house nearly twenty-four hours ago.

"What happened to the shower and change before going to the office?" she asked.

"Didn't happen."

"Obviously."

"Look, if it wouldn't bother you too much, do you think you could be hospitable for a few minutes?"

She crossed her arms over her chest and leaned against the arch separating the foyer from the living room. "I don't know, Garrett," she admitted with a sad smile. "You see, I'm not crazy about being used over and over again by the same man. In fact, I don't like it at all."

Pain and anger flared in his intense gaze. "Good Lord, Megan, I've never meant to hurt you. Everything I did today, I did for you."

"Tell me another one—"

"Damn it, Megan, cut it out! You're not the only one whose reputation has been dragged through the mud, you know."

"But the difference is, *I* know who did the dragging."

Garrett raked tense fingers through his windblown hair. "There are so many things you couldn't possibly understand."

"And maybe I don't want to."

His eyes impaled hers, looking past the pretense of righteous indignation and into the pain beyond her fragile facade. "Oh, God, Megan," he whispered, and his hands dropped to his sides. "I've lost you, haven't I?"

A lump was forming in her throat and her words were choked with the emotion of the last few days. "I think . . . that *lost* is the wrong word. In my opinion, Garrett, you threw me away." Her shoulders slumped and tears pooled in her eyes. "Along with everything we shared."

"You're wrong—"

She put up her palm to interrupt him. "And I always have been, at least when it comes to you." She was shaking by this time, and her slim shoulders moved convulsively as she wrapped her arms around herself. "Don't you understand what I'm trying to say? I'm tired of being used, tired of being a fool for a man who doesn't care for me, tired of being manipulated like some little pawn. It's over, Garrett —if it ever began."

Garrett's jaw worked and his eyes narrowed as he watched her proud display and wondered how much of what she said was from her heart. Without thinking, he crossed the short distance that separated them, took hold of her arm, and pulled her into the living room. Once there, he pushed her into the soft cushions of the couch. "I'm tired and cross—"

"Cross? Tired? You're being incredibly kind to yourself," she snapped, her temper beginning to ignite.

The silent warning in his eyes halted any further interruptions she might have voiced, so she contented herself with staring up at him and soundlessly accusing him of betraying her . . . again.

"I've been on airplanes and in airports for more days than I'd like to count, so it would be wise not to test my patience any further."

Gathering all of her pride, she slowly turned her palm out in his direction. "I'm all ears."

His jaw hardened and he looked as if he wanted to grip her shoulders and shake some sense into her. Instead he walked to the other side of the room and stared for a moment out of the window into the black, cloud-covered morning. "When I left you, I did go back to the apartment," he stated, watching to see if she were bothering to listen. Satisfied that he had her complete attention, he continued. "When I got there, Ron Thurston was there."

Megan nodded, wanting to believe him. The honesty and pain in his stare was beginning to work on her, and all her earlier convictions began to fade.

Garrett continued. "I'd asked Ron to do some digging . . . look into the scam, try to find anything on the swindle, George Samples and you."

Megan stiffened. Ted Benson had warned her that Garrett was looking for skeletons in her closet. She nodded, encouraging him to continue.

Garrett realized that she had known about his private investigation for some time.

"Between what Ron dug up, and what I could piece together myself, I thought that Lana might be involved with the Samples scam."

"But why?" Megan wanted so desperately to believe him, to trust blindly in anything he might say, but she couldn't, not yet. Too many times she had fallen victim to just that trap.

"Because I know my ex-wife and what she's capable of—and because she's done free-lance articles for the *Denver Financial Times* on occasion. I figured George Samples's accomplice had to be someone who wasn't in the office on a day-to-day basis, otherwise the SEC would have been onto the scam the minute it started. Knowing Lana, I put two and two together . . ."

"But your ex-wife—"

"Is not the pillar of virtue she would like everyone to believe." Garrett's eyes darkened dangerously. "There was a time, before we split up, that she lost a very expensive diamond ring. She claimed it was stolen. The insurance paid off to the tune of nearly fifty thousand dollars, and then I found the ring, hidden very neatly in the chandelier. It was a fluke that I found it at all." Garrett's eyebrows had blunted in disgust, and his lips had compressed into a thin, uncompromising line.

Megan felt strangely calm. Listening to Garrett speak of some incident with his ex-wife seemed surprisingly natural. If only she could believe what he was saying.

Garrett walked slowly to the fireplace, propped one foot on the hearth, bent over his knee and stared into Megan's distrustful eyes. "Anyway, to make a long story short, I paid back the insurance money—which by that time Lana had managed to spend. They were satisfied and didn't press charges. So, when I finally got to thinking about this scam, it wasn't too difficult to put two and two together. Ron Thurston hired a private investigator and talked with the SEC. It took a couple of weeks to get the documentation together and prove that Lana was involved, along with this Van Weiss character, who-ever the hell he is."

"You don't know?"

"And I don't want to." Garrett pinched the bridge of his nose between his fingers. "If I had to hazard a guess, I'd bet that Van Weiss is the latest in Lana's string of lovers."

Megan wasn't entirely convinced, though her heart screamed at her to believe him. There were too many unanswered questions. She toyed with the lapel of her robe. "What about today? I saw the paper." She tossed it to him for his perusal, but he set it on the hearth without even the slightest glance at the condemning pages.

"I read the article."

"I think we're still in a lot of trouble. The press is having a field day."

"Let them. Tomorrow—I mean, later today—we'll handle it." Seeing that she was beginning to believe him, if only a little, Garrett sat down on the hearth and held his face in his hands. A low sigh escaped from his lips as he rubbed his forehead.

His bent figure, burdened with sleepless nights and—perhaps—unfair guilt, got to Megan. No matter what had happened, she still loved him, and she couldn't bear to see him suffer.

Casting aside all rational thought, she went to him and placed a comforting hand on the back of his neck. When he looked up, she managed a thin smile. "Don't get me wrong," she whispered, "you still have a lot of explaining to do, but I think you should rest. . . ."

"All I need is a shower and a cup of black coffee," he argued.

"And about forty-eight hours' worth of sleep."

His eyes sought hers. "In time."

"Shhh. . . . I'll start on the coffee. You work on the shower." Tenderly, she placed a kiss on his forehead and was surprised when he reached for her and buried his head in the curve of her neck.

"Thank God you're here," he whispered, his voice thick with unspoken emotions. Then, just as quickly as he had captured her, he let her go.

While Garrett went outside to retrieve the garment bag from his Bronco, Megan started the coffee. She heard him trudge up the stairs, and she listened intently while the water ran in the bathroom.

When he came back downstairs, Garrett looked slightly refreshed. A smile tugged at the corners of his mouth as he surveyed the hearty breakfast she had prepared for him. His shirt gaped open, displaying the hard muscles of his chest. Beads of water still glistened in his ebony hair. His sleeves were rolled over his forearms, and he looked as if he belonged in her home.

"My favorite," he said, nodding at the food. "Thanks." As he sat in one of the cane-backed chairs in the nook, he took a long swallow of the hot coffee. "Aren't you joining me?"

Megan shook her head. "Too early. I'll eat later."

"You'll need some strength to fend off the reporters today."

"And you're going to give it to me—in the form of the truth."

Garrett smiled cryptically and speared a piece of sausage. Within minutes the entire breakfast of sausage, eggs and toast was demolished. Garrett leaned back in his chair, his shirt still open, and set his empty cup on the table.

"You were on the news last night," Megan challenged.

"With Lana." Garrett nodded thoughtfully.

"I don't understand."

"I went to New York. To her town house. And guess who else was there?"

"I couldn't," Megan retorted, her words sounding crisp and dry.

"An investigator from the SEC."

Megan's heart skipped a beat. She took a long, steadying swallow of her coffee as Garrett continued. "I'll admit it was poor timing on my part. Lana practically fell to pieces when she saw me. I stood by her—because she needed my support, not because of any love between us."

Garrett's dark eyes drilled into Megan's and she had to look away. "I told you before that Lana and I never had anything in common. That marriage was the second largest mistake of my life."

"And . . . and the first?"

"Letting you go."

The words echoed in the small room, and Megan felt the sting of tears burning behind her eyelids. How could she love this one man so hopelessly?

Garrett cleared his throat. "Lana made a full confession yesterday, once we got back here and she had talked to Ron Thurston."

"I saw the interview on television. Lana didn't impress me as the type of woman who would fall to pieces."

"She had her act together by the time of the interview, because she knew that if she didn't, it would be all over. Maybe it is anyway. Who knows if this will be a civil suit or a criminal case? I doubt that Ron will be able to protect her much."

"Oh, God, Garrett, this whole business is just such a mess." Megan rubbed her arms as if to ward off a sudden chill. "Why did they have to pick McKearn Investments in the first place?"

"Simple. George Samples worked for McKearn. Basically, it was nothing against you. You just got in the way."

Megan's eyebrow lifted in doubt. "Is that so? Well, since you seem to be the man with all of the answers today, why don't you tell me how George got involved and why you were one of the clients singled out to be part of the scam? Why your account? No matter what *your* story is, you'll probably have to convince the SEC that your ex-wife didn't give you the inside information before the articles hit the papers."

"I already have."

"What? When?"

"Lana may be a lot of things, but she wouldn't let me take the fall for this. Not now. Oh, she might have if Van Weiss and Samples had pressured her, but I was there when the SEC came down on her, and she assured them that I wasn't a part of the plan."

"Do they believe her?"

Dark eyes glinted. "Do you?"

Megan paused. The clock ticked off the silent seconds as her eyes reached into his. "I've never wanted to believe anything more in my life."

"But you don't . . ."

Megan shook her head. "I know it's illogical and crazy and absolutely ridiculous, but I do believe you, Garrett. Why, I don't know."

"Because it's the truth." He pushed the chair away from the table. It scraped against the hardwood floor as he stood. "Megan, everything I've done was to insure that you and I will be able to start again—without the yoke of past or present scandals to burden our relationship."

He reached for her, and the gentle touch of his fingers against her face made her knees grow weak.

"Just trust me."

She didn't pull away from the pleasure of his touch. Instead, she looked into his eyes. "But what about George. Why did he involve you? It doesn't make any sense."

"Remember what I told you before—about George protecting himself and hedging his bets?"

Megan nodded, encouraging him to explain himself. Garrett smiled, and his finger slowly slid down her throat until her heart began to beat in a faster cadence.

"That was only part of his plan. According to Lana, he wanted to make a lot of money for my account because he was hoping to be in my good graces. He was planning to take a job at a rival brokerage house and steal accounts away from McKearn Investments. You see, my darling, George Samples had reconciled himself to the fact that he couldn't work with you. He knew that either he would be fired or he would quit, whichever came first. When you stumbled onto his scam, he wasn't left with much of a choice.

"My guess is that he would have involved other large accounts in the swindle in hopes of taking them with him when he left, but he didn't get the chance."

Garrett's arms encircled her and Megan didn't pull away. She rested her head against his chest and listened to the rhythmic hammering of his heart. It was so warm in the protection of his arms. It felt so right. As if she belonged.

"So what do we do now?" she asked as her arms fitted around his waist.

He placed both of his hands on her chin and forced her to look into the wisdom of his eyes. "What we should have done long ago."

"Which is?"

"I love you, Megan," he whispered. "I want you to marry me." He reached into his pocket and extracted a gold ring with a solitary diamond. "Will you be my wife?"

Megan swallowed back her tears of joy. "Don't you think we should wait—"

"We have." Garrett gently nudged her neck. "Three years is long enough. And don't give me any business-before-pleasure garbage, because I won't buy it. You and I both know that we'll be able to face the press, come what may. My guess is that the Securities and Exchange Commission will have this case wrapped up by the end of the week, and that you and I, lady, will be off scot-free."

"You think so?"

He placed a kiss of promise on her parted lips. "I guarantee it."

"A few hours ago I was ready to purge you from my life."

His lips brushed seductively over hers. "I would have convinced you otherwise—"

"Sure of yourself, aren't you?"

"I just know that I love you and that you, dear one, whether you admit it or not, feel the same about me. So—"his finger slid between the lapels of her robe"—what do you say?"

Megan smiled through the shimmer of her tears. All of her doubts had disappeared into the mists of the past. "Of course I'll marry you," she whispered hoarsely.

With a glint of satisfaction lighting his eyes, Garrett slipped the ring on her finger. He bent and caught her knees with the crook of his arm, lifting her off her feet. "It's still early," he explained, "and you and I have a lot of catching up to do."

"I'm all yours . . ."

"Thank God," he whispered fervently. "This time it's forever."

ENTER:

Here's your chance to win a fabulous $50,000 diamond jewelry collection, consisting of diamond necklace, bracelet, earrings and ring.

All you have to do to enter is fill out the coupon below and mail it by September 30, 1985.

Send entries to:

In the U.S.	Silhouette Diamond Sweepstakes P.O. Box 779 Madison Square Station New York, NY 10159
In Canada	Silhouette Diamond Sweepstakes Suite 191 238 Davenport Road Toronto, Ontario M5R 1J6

NAME_____

ADDRESS_____

CITY_____ STATE/(PROV.)_____

ZIP/(POSTAL CODE)_____

BCD-A-1

RULES FOR SILHOUETTE DIAMOND SWEEPSTAKES

OFFICIAL RULES—NO PURCHASE NECESSARY

1. Silhouette Diamond Sweepstakes is open to Canadian (except Quebec) and United States residents 18 years or older at the time of entry. Employees and immediate families of the publishers of Silhouette, their affiliates, retailers, distributors, printers, agencies and RONALD SMILEY INC. are excluded.

2. To enter, print your name and address on the official entry form or on a 3" x 5" slip of paper. You may enter as often as you choose, but each envelope must contain only one entry. Mail entries first class in Canada to Silhouette Diamond Sweepstakes, Suite 191, 238 Davenport Road, Toronto, Ontario M5R 1J6. In the United States, mail to Silhouette Diamond Sweepstakes, P.O. Box 779, Madison Square Station, New York, NY 10159. Entries must be postmarked between February 1 and September 30, 1985. Silhouette is not responsible for lost, late or misdirected mail.

3. First Prize of diamond jewelry, consisting of a necklace, ring, bracelet and earrings will be awarded. Approximate retail value is $50,000 U.S./$62,500 Canadian. Second Prize of 100 Silhouette Home Reader Service Subscriptions will be awarded. Approximate retail value of each is $162.00 U.S./$180.00 Canadian. No substitution, duplication, cash redemption or transfer of prizes will be permitted. Odds of winning depend upon the number of valid entries received. One prize to a family or household. Income taxes, other taxes and insurance on First Prize are the sole responsibility of the winners.

4. Winners will be selected under the supervision of RONALD SMILEY INC., an independent judging organization whose decisions are final, by random drawings from valid entries postmarked by September 30, 1985, and received no later than October 7, 1985. Entry in this sweepstakes indicates your awareness of the Official Rules. Winners who are residents of Canada must answer correctly a time-related arithmetical skill-testing question to qualify. First Prize winner will be notified by certified mail and must submit an Affidavit of Compliance within 10 days of notification. Returned Affidavits or prizes that are refused or undeliverable will result in alternative names being randomly drawn. Winners may be asked for use of their name and photo at no additional compensation.

5. For a First Prize winner list, send a stamped self-addressed envelope postmarked by September 30, 1985. In Canada, mail to Silhouette Diamond Contest Winner, Suite 309, 238 Davenport Road, Toronto, Ontario M5R 1J6. In the United States, mail to Silhouette Diamond Contest Winner, P.O. Box 182, Bowling Green Station, New York, NY 10274. This offer will appear in Silhouette publications and at participating retailers. Offer void in Quebec and subject to all Federal, Provincial, State and Municipal laws and regulations and wherever prohibited or restricted by law.

Silhouette Special Edition. Romances for the woman who expects a little more out of love.

If you enjoyed this book, and you're ready for more great romance

...get 4 romance novels FREE when you become a Silhouette Special Edition home subscriber.

Act now and we'll send you four exciting Silhouette Special Edition romance novels. They're our gift to introduce you to our convenient home subscription service. Every month, we'll send you six new passion-filled Special Edition books. Look them over for 15 days. If you keep them, pay just $11.70 for all six. Or return them at no charge.

We'll mail your books to you two full months *before they are available anywhere else.* Plus, with every shipment, you'll receive the Silhouette Books Newsletter absolutely free. *And with Silhouette Special Edition there are never any shipping or handling charges.*

Mail the coupon today to get your four free books—and more romance than you ever bargained for.

MAIL THIS COUPON
and get 4 thrilling

Silhouette Desire®

novels <u>FREE</u> (a $7.80 value)

Silhouette Desire books may not be for everyone. They *are* for readers who want a sensual, provocative romance. These are modern love stories that are charged with emotion from the first page to the thrilling happy ending—about women who discover the extremes of fiery passion. Confident women who face the challenge of today's world and overcome all obstacles to attain their dreams—*and their desires.*

We believe you'll be so delighted with Silhouette Desire romance novels that you'll want to receive them regularly through our home subscription service. Your books will be *shipped to you two months before they're available anywhere else*—so you'll never miss a new title. Each month we'll send you 6 new books to look over for 15 days, without obligation. If not delighted, simply return them and owe nothing. Or keep them and pay only $1.95 each. There's no charge for postage or handling. And there's no obligation to buy anything at any time. You'll also receive a subscription to the Silhouette Books Newsletter *absolutely free!*

So don't wait. To receive your four FREE books, fill out and mail the coupon below *today!*

SILHOUETTE DESIRE and colophon are registered trademarks and a service mark.

Silhouette Desire,® 120 Brighton Road, P.O. Box 5084, Clifton, N.J. 07015-5084

Yes, please send me FREE and without obligation, 4 exciting Silhouette Desire books. Unless you hear from me after I receive them, send me 6 new Silhouette Desire books to preview each month before they're available anywhere else. I understand that you will bill me just $1.95 each for a total of $11.70—with no additional shipping, handling or other hidden charges. **There is no minimum number of books that I must buy, and I can cancel anytime I wish.** The first 4 books are mine to keep, even if I never take a single additional book.

☐ Mrs. ☐ Miss ☐ Ms. ☐ Mr.   BDS2R5

Name	*(please print)*
Address	Apt. #
City	State Zip
( ) Area Code	Telephone Number

Signature (If under 18, parent or guardian must sign.)

This offer limited to one per customer. Terms and prices subject to change. Your enrollment is subject to acceptance by Silhouette Books.

D-OP-A